MOVING WEST,
as told by
GILBERT CLOCK

Book 2 of the Trilogy
"Every Hour Counts"

Thomas J Ault

J. Jessica from Tom Ault

Other Books By Author:
Children's Books:

My Name is Jake
Jake's World of Flowers
Jake's Animal Friends
Jake's Nature Walk
Jake's Feather Friends
Jake's Travels
Jake's New Friends

Family Oriented:

Every Hour Counts

Mystery:

The Incident

Special Thanks to
Paulette, my wife,
who has put up with me this year during the
writing of the book.
Also I would like to acknowledge
Jim and Mary Kennedy,
who continue to encourage me,
and to
The Wikipedia and The
Council Bluffs, Iowa Historical Society,
from which many of the facts have been gleened,
and, last but not least,
my ancestors, upon which, much of this book's
background has been based.

Prologue

It is 1908 and Don and Molly have returned from New York! It seems like I have waited forever for them to come back from, what they described to everyone as, their exciting trip. They were only gone a few days but it seemed forever to me. Thank goodness they wound me before leaving so my life wasn't put on hold while they were gone!

I have been waiting, and rather impatiently I might add, to hear more about that large ball that was being dropped from the sky and the other exciting news about their trip. There have been rumors of their moving away, and I hoped that would not materialize.

Imagine being uprooted and moved to some wild place where Indians (whatever they are) were roaming about. Being just a clock, with no one to protect me, an Indian might like to use me to start a fire. Hopefully, these were just exaggerated conversations between the family members, and not real plans for the future.

CHAPTER 1

"Don, it is so-o-o good to be home; but we did have a wonderful time, didn't we?"

"Of course we did Molly. It reminded me of our courting days, with bringing in the new year of 1908 at Times Square in New York City added for good measure."

Molly gave him a smack on the cheek. "You are so imaginative, but wonderfully so."

They removed their winter outerwear, and hung them on the clothes hooks inside the kitchen door before they came into the den.

Don asked, "How about a fire, a brandy for me, and maybe hot tea for you?"

Molly went into the kitchen to get some water knowing that Don would build a fire and soon the den would be inviting. How fortunate they were that their wonderful neighbor had started a fire in the furnace so the house was already warm and cozy, rather than having succumbed to the bitter cold outside. Don opened the door of the wood box and found the stash of small kindling pieces left over from last week. He removed several sticks and stacked them in a pyramid shape, then returned to a larger box and pulled out three nicely hewn blocks of wood to burn. He was quite the expert when it came to stoking a fire, and his ability was admired by everyone who was fortunate enough to be invited to his and Molly's home.

"The fire looks wonderful, Don." She brought the water from the kitchen and put it into the hanging kettle. "Heating it with the swing catch will work fine, and it will be cozier than heating it in the kitchen."

"That's a great idea, hon."

Don assumed his accustomed stance at the fireplace with one foot on the hearth, a glass of brandy in his hand, and a desired air of aristocracy. Fortunately, Molly had a way of keeping his imagination from getting out of hand.

Molly smirked. "You do look very elegant, but did you notice that you have soot on your face?"

"Soot," Don questioned? He tried to wipe away the smear that he was told was there, without much success.

She answered him with a bit of sarcasm in her voice. "Yes soot. You probably rubbed your cheek after setting up the fire. It sure takes away from the suave appearance you are trying to achieve."

"Now Molly...," he acted as though he was offended.

"That's all right sweetheart, you have every right to look snooty occasionally; everyone gets to pretend from time to time, even me."

They both laughed at the situation as Don removed a handkerchief from his pocket, and wiped his face. He carefully replaced the handkerchief then took a sip of his drink. Molly got up from where she had been sitting and walked to the fireplace and removed her kettle from the keeper. She filled the brass tea dispenser with tealeaves and placed it into the kettle for steeping.

"I was thinking how nice it would be to have a few guests over and tell them about our trip. What do you think?"

"Sounds splendid to me, just family and friends. When do you want to do that?"

Molly turned her head slightly, pursed her lips, and after careful consideration, she suggested that they should get settled first.

"How about the 10th of the month? That would be next Friday night and would give us a week to prepare"

Don seemed to question the timing. "If you feel that gives enough time to get our clothes washed and ironed, and everything else straightened away." *He paused, giving it a second thought.* "But, with only a week to plan, and get the invitations ready, will that be enough time?"

Molly, continuing her own thoughts, acted as though he had not spoken. "I think we should invite all of our friends. What do you think?"

Then realizing what he said, she continued without waiting for an answer to his question. "I don't think we have to be that perfect in our etiquette this time Don, and you're right, we should just invite family and close friends."

The date of January 10 was established and, as always, it would be at seven o'clock in the evening and after the dinner hour. Don walked over to the window and looked out. He saw a slight dusting of snow on the ground as night started to fall. The trip had been an exciting one but it ended all too quickly; unfortunately there was his job to return to. His jaw dropped at the thought.

Don took a sip of his brandy, "You're right, formality is not required. We can use that new telephone and handle the invitations quickly. Good thinking! I never seem to remember that we have the darn apparatus!"

Molly was surprised at his language and stared at him in surprise.

"Don, you know we don't use that word here. That apparatus is called a telephone, without expletives, and we should acknowledge that, don't you agree?

Don turned toward his lovely wife, and while appearing to study the floor, he quietly answered.

"I'm sorry, that was a slip of the tongue, I won't let it happen again, please forgive me."

Molly smiled, and in her gracious way, acknowledged his apology. They left me alone in the den and hand in hand they walked through the doorway to the hall. I was certain that after the day they have had, they will sleep soundly.

CHAPTER 2

I heard Molly as she awoke early. She muttered sleepily to Don that she had a busy week ahead. I imagined her getting up, with her nightgown wrinkled, and pulling the sleeves down around her wrists as she yawned, stretched, and looked at Don, who was probably still half-asleep.

"Another day honey, time to get up."

I could hear him as he used the side of the mattress for leverage to get up. He must have sat with his feet not reaching the cold floor, since I did not hear them touch it.

Shivering, he answered, "You are so right, another day at the factory. Sometimes I wish I was ready to retire. It seems that the days get longer, the work more grueling, and the problems more difficult. I remember when I used to look forward to getting up and facing another challenge. Do you think old age is catching me?"

Molly giggled as she tormented, "The only thing that is catching you is lack of ambition. Come on now, you know how important it is for you to be on time for work. You must set a good example for that young Mr. Weatherby. If you want to retire and have him replace you one day, you must train him properly."

Don raised his hands to his face and rubbed the night-salt from his eyes. "Of course you are right, but…"

Molly interrupted, "There are no "but's" about it. Now you get ready for work while I start our breakfast."

I could hear the sound of pots and pans being moved about as she searched for the iron skillet she would use for preparing their breakfast. The aroma of tea being steeped and eggs being fried filled the air. The house was warm and loving again. It was so good have them home once more.

Being a clock can be difficult from time to time. Every one relies on me to be accurate. So few humans recognize that we clocks have to be taken care of too, we need oiling, cleaning, winding, dusting, and polishing. Some folks neglect us totally and still expect us to perform. I am fortunate that Molly will be coming in soon to clean and polish my finish. Her touch feels the same to me as it did in the first house, when she would coo over me like a long lost friend. Her warm hand is still so wonderful.

"Don," Molly called from the base of the stairs, "breakfast is ready."
"Okay Molly, I'm coming. I have to put on my shoes and I'll be there."

I could hear the clump, clump, clump coming down the stairs. It always sounded so loud, but the stairs do tend to cause an echo. They even enhance the sound of my chimes.

As Don entered the kitchen, he embraced her and he loudly proclaimed,

"Molly, this smells wonderful. It makes me feel glad to be home where I can enjoy your wonderful cooking."

She looked at him tauntingly, "Don't spread it on too thick! I might become snooty."
They sat down and held hands across the table as Don said the morning prayer.

"Dear heavenly Father, we come to you to say thanks for the safe journey that we have returned from. We also thank you for the loving care you have bestowed upon our home. We ask that you bless our home, our family wherever they may be today, and please bless this food to our needs. Amen."

Each day was started the same way. Don and Molly have done this every day that I have been with them. I always wondered if there were clocks in heaven too. I fear that when our usefulness is no longer a value to our owners, all that will be in store for us is the trash heap. Then again, I feel this will not

Be the case. I am with a family that loves me, and cares for me as a clock should be cared for. In return I try to repay that love by being correct with the time when it is needed. I think I shall always be needed, both here and beyond.

"Don, I am still considering who to invite this coming Friday. I know that I had said "everyone", but that would be an awfully large group. Do you have any suggestions?"

"You know I don't normally get involved in that. It is nice to be asked, but my list would be quite short and probably end with the Hillmans and the Newsomes? Any one you feel you would like to invite is fine with me."

Molly pulled a piece of paper from the counter top as she answered him, "I will put them first on the list. Maybe Margaret would like to help me. She knows everyone we know, and she always helps with the parties we have."

"Sounds great. She is such an asset to you, and a wonderful neighbor as well."

I heard him get up from his chair, and start walking toward the door as Molly reminded him, "Don't forget to ask your assistant if he and his wife would like to come."

He walked back to the table and told her, "I won't forget. Now give me a kiss so I can get going. I'm already late, and you know the tin lizzy may not start right away."

I heard him give her a peck on the cheek, pull his hat and over-coat from the peg beside the side door, and leave closing the door behind him. I anticipated that since he was forgetful at times, he would soon rush back inside, take off his outer coat, dash up the stairs, put on his tie, pull on his suit coat, and button its top button. He would then rush back down the stairs, grabbing his hat and outer coat once again, and then burst out of the door! This was always 'Act I' in the shows that I have witnessed since I first came to live with the Holscombs. The slam of the side door was the finale of the great show, and the imagined crowd would sit in awe. (Of course, the crowd was just Molly and me)

Even with the door closed to the outside I could hear Don turning the crank on the front of his tin lizzy. It always took more than one turn, the engine would backfire, and then Don would say something inaudible to my hearing. (I was glad it was, since when he spoke loudly, his language was less than flattering, especially when turning the engine crank.

This time the play did not end as usual. Don was dressed and prepared to leave from the kitchen. As much as I missed the show, it was good to know that he was ready to attack the workload that lay in front of him at his office.

CHAPTER 3

The dishes clanged as Molly dried and put them away. Soon she had the early morning chores out of the way and hoped that Margaret, her next-door neighbor would suddenly appear.

Molly opened the kitchen door and discovered that her wish had come true.

"Hello, anybody home?"

"I was just thinking of you Margaret. Come on in, I have a lot to tell you."

Molly knew that her neighbor would be dying to hear about the latest news of her trip to New York. She wanted to tell her about the dropping of the ball in Times Square, and of course, any other juicy tidbits that might be worth mentioning.

"I bet you're glad to get home, aren't you?"

"Well," Molly answered, "yes and no."

"Yes and no?" Margaret found that confusing.

"Yes, it is always good to get back to your own place, your own bed, and the comforts of home."

She examined the "yes and no" comment she had just made, then explained the "no" part.

"Then there is "no, I am not glad" because New York has so many things to see, and remembering all the things we did while all the time knowing there was so much more to do."

Margaret was excited, "I guess that would be the "no" part alright. I can't wait to hear about it."

The teapot was on, as it usually was at this time of morning, so they poured their tea, then both, with their apron strings tied neatly behind them came back into the parlor, where they were primed to talk about the happenings of the last few days.

There was always something new to talk about when either of them had been gone, and this was very special, since Margaret had been waiting to hear of the trip, and the greatly anticipated gossip of New York. Molly was excited as she talked to her friend.

"We went by train, of course you already knew that."

Margaret nodded yes.

"We were met by no less than," she giggled and her face flushed slightly, "the engineer that designed the New York Subways, Bill Parsons and his wife Polly."

Molly put her hand on her cheek and looked at the ceiling.

"What a lovely person she was."

Margaret could hardly sit still, "Was she wearing something spectacular?"

"No, as a matter of fact, she was dressed quite plainly. I was so glad there were no pretenses; it made me feel comfortable. She wore a very plain black satin dress. It came just below the knee and had some kind of fur trim around the bottom at the hem. It was tight around the middle and had a slight flair just above the trim. The white lace at the top was high on the throat and there was just enough room for the beautiful oval pin that I think was made of porcelain and decorated with a dainty hand painted flower. She had a beautiful ostrich plumed hat with smaller feathers on the side. They appeared to be from either a pheasant or a rough grouse."

"I thought you said she was dressed rather simply?" Margaret interrupted.

"Well, for a person of her station, and living in New York? I thought it was quite simple. Of course it was the latest style, especially with those high- heeled shoes. They must have been at least three inches high!"

Margaret exclaimed, "She must have stood out in the crowd! That sounds pretty fancy to me."

As an afterthought Molly answered, "I suppose, now that I think about it, she was dressed nicely, but she wasn't a bit pretentious."

"Did they meet you with some new and fancy conveyance?"

"Yes, they did. I think they called it a limousine. It was quite long and black, and could carry several people but there were just five of us. Did I tell you that General Dodge was there as well?"

"General Dodge, wasn't that the gentleman that Don went to see when you were in Iowa?"

"Yes, one and the same; as you may remember, he is a railroad mogul. He and Mr. Parsons have a lot in common."

Margaret sat glued to her chair in anticipation of hearing more about the adventure as Molly giggled, and continued, telling her about the limousine.

"It had so much room that we all sat comfortably. Just sitting next to these important people, and in such a fine motorcar was exhilarating, especially when the driver took us through part of Central Park. Everyone just stared at us as we drove by."

Margaret's eyes opened wider than before when she asked, "Did you wave at them?"

Molly blushed, "Of course not, that would have been bad behavior, wouldn't it?"

Molly readily decided Margaret was only teasing. Without waiting for some silly answer, she continued.

"You would not believe how big and special that place is, unless you could see it for yourself. It had gaslights on all the roads and paths, so that folks could enjoy the place, even at night. It was such a wondrous sight."

"Weren't you frightened, being in that big place at night?" Margaret inquired.

"We didn't go to places where those gangs that we have read about live. We stayed close to the park and our hotel, even while in the limousine, besides, Mrs. Parsons and I were with Don and two other strong men, plus the driver of the motorcar."

Changing the subject, Margaret asked, "I hear the restaurants are getting all white tile floors now, a kind of cleanliness thing. Did you see any of that?"

"Oh yes. That seems to be the rage now, black and white tile floors. They are beautiful, but I sure wouldn't want to have to wash them."

Molly and Margaret giggled at the thought of their washing them.

"Did you see the Waldorf Astoria Hotel?"

"We not only saw it, that is where we stayed."

"Now I am getting jealous. Did you attend their high tea too?"

Molly raised her hand, then she slightly bent her little finger as though holding a fancy teacup. She raised her eyebrows exposing those beautiful eyes, and attempted to be a snob.

"Of course my darling, we attended the Saturday afternoon tea. Anyone of taste would, you know."

Margaret looked at her and laughed knowing that Molly was teasing her, and then she leaned more heavily on the table with both arms.

"Tell me more."

Molly pulled a rolled-up paper from a kitchen drawer and handed it to Margaret.

"Well, this is what I brought you."

It was an announcement about the tea, and in its special typeset made it a true souvenir.

1906 AFTERNOON TEA
HAS BECOME SO FASHIONABLE
THAT NYC'S WALDORF-ASTORIA SUPPLEMENTS
THE WALDORF GARDEN SPACE BY OPENING
THE EMPIRE ROOM
FROM 4 TO 6 P.M. – FOR LUNCH
YOU MAY WISH TO INVESTIGATE ITALIAN-AMERICANS
LUISA AND GEROME LEONE AT THEIR
SMALL TABLE D'HOTE RESTAURANT
IN NYC NEAR THE METROPOLITAN OPERA.

Margaret read the announcement and then she laid the paper on the table. She stretched toward the center of the table and curved her finger in imitation of what Molly had done earlier.

Before she could ask for anything, Molly took the hint and reacted to her friend's silliness.

"If you would care to join me now, perhaps you would enjoy my special tea, imported from downtown Waterbury, and home-made sugar cookies?"

The friends laughed as Molly poured the second cup of tea and their conversation continued about the New York trip, the dropping of the large seventy-pound ball, and the many other sights that Molly had seen.

With no more to be said, Molly ended the description of her trip. They sat and enjoyed their tea and cookies as their individual imaginations took them to their own special wonderland.

CHAPTER 4

"Margaret, we are planning to have a gathering of friends, and I was hoping that you could help me with the list. You know everyone we know, and I don't want to hurt anyone's feelings, but I don't want to invite too many either. Do you have some suggestions?"

Molly stood and walked to the counter where she kept a few pieces of paper, cut into small sizes, for note keeping.

"I think these will help. We can write the names down, and we'll decide if there is anyone that I would rather not have, well at least at the same time as some others. How many people do you think I should consider?"

"Maybe fifteen or so, including us, that should be enough. What do you think?"

"Sounds fine to me, I wouldn't want it to be one of those stuffy affairs that no one enjoys."

"Okay, let's start. How about starting with Reverend Hardcore and his wife, Lydia?"
Margaret thought for a few seconds before replying.

"Do you think that they would be able to come now since they moved some distance away? They are getting on in years."

Margaret thought about it for a second, then answered, "You could be right. Let's write them in as tentative. I know how much that you love them, but you could be right, an evening trip may be quite tiring for them."

She continued, "How about Mrs. Benson? She was your midwife you know."

"Okay, let's put her down. Does she have a husband?"

Margaret was puzzled, "I don't think so." She hesitated and then resumed her thought, "I am sure you want your brother-in-law and his wife to come. Do you want the boys as well?"

"Good question. They have become young men now and probably have no desire to sit around with a bunch of old fogies like us. Let's just leave it open. They can come if they want to, but they don't have to."

"I think that makes perfect sense. These youngsters today have a mind of their own, especially those in their high-school years."

The morning disappeared and noon came rather quickly. Margaret went home and I could hear Molly in the kitchen fixing lunch. It was nice hearing her there, after being alone for a few days. Even we clocks get lonesome when the house is silent except for our loud ticking while gonging the hours away. It wasn't long until she came into the den with a soft cloth with oil on it. I knew it was time for my cleaning and polishing and I longed for her touch.

When she finished brightening my wooded body, she left the room and returned, still with her apron tied neatly around her. She had the guest list in her hand and headed toward the hall where the phone hung on the wall. She hit the little catch on the side a couple of times and the barely inaudible voice of the operator could be heard in the den.

"Yes Mrs. Holscomb, what number would you like?"

"Hello Matilda. How are you today?"

"Been real busy lately, a lot of phone calls being made. I hope someday they come up with a simpler method of handling so many calls."

"But Matilda," Molly teased, "look at it this way, we wouldn't know what was going on around here if it wasn't for you."

"Are you saying I listen to everything?"

Molly knew right then and there that she had said the wrong thing.

"I didn't mean that you were…" Matilda interrupted, "A busybody?"

"No, that wasn't what I was going to say."

Matilda charged again, "Then what was it?"

Molly was getting in deeper and deeper, but I knew that she was trying to say something nice to the operator.

"Matilda, I am sorry. I really didn't mean to offend you. I merely meant that you get to know everyone, just like you knew me when you pushed that thingy into the hole in your switchboard."

"Look Mrs. Holscomb, I am sorry. I have had a bad morning; just got off the line with someone who called me a nosy busybody and know- it-all gossiper. That hurt my feelings and I just took it out on you. Please forgive me?"

Molly, in her gentle manner, accepted the apology on the phone. I have heard her soothe many ruffled feathers in the past. It's in her nature and who would know better than I, since I am here all the time with her? I feel that I know her better than anyone, except Don, of course!

"I forgive you Matilda and I'm sorry about what I said. I shouldn't tease. I hate to burden you with this, but I have quite a list of numbers to call. We are having a small gathering of friends and decided to invite them using the phone instead of sending out invitations. Let me start with," she hesitated a second, "why not start with you? Would you like to come to our home and hear about our trip to New York?"

Matilda, taken by surprise at the invitation responded, "I don't know. We have never met, are you sure you want me to come?"

Molly, knowing Matilda was right, but having no choice now, continued, stuttering some, "Of course I do, or I wouldn't have asked."

Matilda, knowing the stuttering was a reflex, answered, "What night would that be?"

Molly looked at her calendar that hung on the wall close by the phone. "Friday, the 10th."

Matilda cleverly turned down the invitation knowing the invitation was a slip of the tongue on Molly's part.

"Oh, I'm sorry. I wish I could come, but I have to be on this switchboard until nine when we close. I can't come."

Molly was relieved, but did not let on. "I'm so sorry. It would have been wonderful to meet you, and have you meet some of the folks you talk to. Maybe you can make it the next time; for now, let's start calling with number 22."

The next hour, or so, was spent with Molly on the phone talking to this person and that person, until she had completed her list. The list included Mrs. Benson, the midwife for Catherine's birth, Suzanne and Sam Briggs, even though he did tend to drink a bit and she was snobby from time to time, Brenda and Ward Hillman, the folks that own the brewery, John and Shirley Newsome from the new UPS office,

Louise Thatcher and her husband Richard, who was Don's boss, Rick and Angela Weatherby, Don's apprentice and wife, and last but not least, George and Margaret Billings from next door.

Later I heard Don' voice, echo from the kitchen door.

"Hello Molly, I 'm home."

"I heard you drive up." Molly answered.

They met, , right in front of the den door, he coming from the side door and she from the parlor. I could feel the strong hug, and hear a kiss on his cheek. Their love never failed to amaze me, let alone make me wish at times that I could be human and have someone to hug, and have the arms to do it with.

"I had a great day today, how about you?"

"It was all right I guess, just another day at the office, if you know what I mean."

"That's it? Just another day at the office! I thought it would have been a great day with you telling the others about your trip, and how well the company's largest account was doing in New York."

Molly was a bit dismayed at his answer.

"Well, Rick became ill over the weekend and did not come in today, Richard acted like a trip to New York was nothing, and I suppose that for him it wasn't. My work had piled up although I only took off a day or so.

Consequently, I worked my fingers to the bone all day on a project, just to have it fall through at the last minute. I can honestly say, it was not a good day at the office."

"I'm sorry it was so bad honey. Why don't you fix your usual, start a fire in the fireplace, and I'll be back in a minute or two, after I get dinner started?"

Don was grateful for her devotion. "I don't know what I would do without you Molly. You are, without doubt, the most thoughtful person in the world. Why you put up with me, at times like this, is more than I can imagine."

Molly set off for the kitchen while Don opened the cabinet door and plucked his favorite brandy from the shelf. He removed his snifter from its special shelf and poured it three quarters full. Even for him, that was more than enough brandy. Finally, when he had settled his nerves, he started the fire and waited for Molly.

Calling from the kitchen, Molly asked, "What do you think happened today when I called our friends to come to our little get-together?"

Don answered between sips, "I don't know, hon, what happened?"

Molly came back down the hallway to the den and sat on the settee across from Don's big chair where he sat sipping his drink.

"Everyone agreed to come, but I did a very foolish thing before I got everyone called."

"What was that?"

"I upset our phone operator. She thought I called her a busybody."

"Why would she think that for goodness sake? You never speak badly about anyone!"

Molly proceeded to tell Don what had transpired, almost tearfully at times. He listened intently, then he smiled broadly as he told her that the switchboard operator probably was a busy body, and she probably did know everyone's business. He told her that he was glad the operator wasn't' coming to the party because, as he put it, "she would learn too much and would undoubtedly tell everyone about it."

"Don, you should be ashamed of yourself."

Don replied, "No, I don't think so, that was my belief when we first got the darned apparatus and I doubt I shall change my mind!"

Molly gave Don a look that said, "shame on you." Don took another sip of his drink as the fire jumped and flashed its red and gold colors.

The evening changed into night as the dinner readied itself over the hot stove's burners. It was another night that ended with happiness between the two.

CHAPTER 5

The days passed swiftly, and Friday the 10th came before anyone realized that the week had gone by. The party arrangements had all been completed, and the house was clean and fresh. Don stoked the furnace when he came home from the office as Molly prepared for their guests. All was right with the world.

Their dinner was quick but substantial. It was Don's favorite meal, a wonderful stew of roast beef, carrots, boiled potatoes, some onion, and celery.

She reserved her marvelous tasting bread pudding for the dessert to be served later that night with her special raison sauce.

When the dinner was over, Don and Molly finished washing and drying the dishes. George and Margaret arrived to help set up the den with napkins and tooth- picks for the finger foods.

As always, there were wine glasses for the red or white wine of choice, and three or four brandy snifters for those who would indulge themselves later with Don.

The ladies would enjoy any new gossip of the day while savoring their hot tea.

The knocker offered its first friendly sound of the evening announcing that John and Shirley Newsom had arrived. I waited impatiently to hear some new and fascinating discussion, probably about politics. It was equally interesting for me to see how his wife Shirley would, in her teasing way, get the other guests started on some unimportant subject and then simply disappear from the discussion knowing it would lead to a serious debate between those she left behind

John shook Don's hand vigorously. "We are glad to be here. Shirley is looking forward to hearing about New York, and so am I."

"I don't recall telling John we were going to hear about New York. I did discuss it with Molly though. Do you think John might be psychic?"

She winked at Molly as she said it. I could see that Shirley had already set the pace for the evening discussions. I had little doubt that poor John could be the recipient of her ridicule. She removed her stole and coat, then she handed them to Don.

Changing the subject, Don asked, "How is that new business going John? Strong I hope."

"It's going along smoothly, although not as fast as I would like; but it is getting there."

Don continued his line of questioning, "Have you been getting increased business through the holidays?"

John looked at the floor as he contemplated his answer, "Yes, I think so. Our figures are showing that December was about twenty percent more than November. Of course, according to what we have been told, November is a strong month due to shipping being done in time for Christmas. December hopefully catches up the late shoppers, and also those out of town deliveries that sometimes are incorrectly shipped or occasionally mislabeled."

Don accepted the answer as he poured a brandy for his friend and himself. "I see."

"Does this mean that January, having no holiday to fall back on, could be slower than you would like?"

"That is a possibility, but I don't have any figures yet, so I must assume that as people are recuperating from the holidays, returning from trips, and consequently not spending much on shipping, things could slow down."

Don suggested more commercial business might be the answer and John agreed. "You're right. I have contacted many companies around here that are shipping goods. I even contacted your parts people again this week, and they told me that you have not been getting as many orders to ship as last year."

Don took a sip of his drink, and then from his usual stance at the fireplace he answered, "Unfortunately that is correct. We have completed several large projects and have suggested inventories of spare parts, which they have gone along with, but unfortunately for you, and for us, they have asked us to keep them in our warehouse until they need them. Now we have an overload of product and a shortage of space. At the same time, we have a lot of happy customers. We handle their storage, but at least the product is sold."

John took a heavy drink from his snifter. As he started to make another point, the knocker again bounced against the doorplate announcing that more guests had arrived. Molly opened the door to find Brenda and Ward Hillman standing in wait. Ward, with his usual guttural outburst, hugged her as he entered the door.

"I declare, Molly, you look younger and younger. I think the trip to New York City has done you a lot of good. I only wish something would do the same for me!"

Wards wife Brenda spoke, much more softly, but not with less proficiently.

"I don't do as well with words, but I do think you look marvelous, but I think I should just accept a kiss on both cheeks. A hug lacks the etiquette that we must adhere to."

"You two are wonderful, even though you are perhaps a bit gregarious, from a social point of view that is." Molly smiled, took their coats, and continued, "As always, we are so glad you could come."

"Not nearly as glad as I am." Ward spoke out with his guttural voice.

"Just getting to be with someone other than this wife of mine is meaningful to me."

Brenda spoke up, pointing a finger, and with an authoritative voice she gave him a directive. "Ward, don't get too personal, just be a gentleman tonight, for a change!"

I could see that this might be an entertaining night, even though stressful for some. I may learn a lot more about these folks, maybe more than I should! It was not long before all of the guests had arrived, except Don's brother and wife, and his assistant and his wife. Don decided to start the conversations without them.

"Welcome to our home again,. We are so glad to see you. It's been a while since you have all been here at the same time. I think you all know each other except for the owner of The Brass Company. Allow me to introduce the president of our company, Mr. Richard Thatcher, and his lovely wife, Louise."

Mr. Thatcher put his hand in the air to identify himself as he moved to the center of the room with Louise. They were a charming couple and dressed befitting the president of The Brass Company and his wife.

He was a striking six-footer, plus or minus an inch, and had a well-built body. His shoulders were quite wide and his waist narrowed at the middle. His jaw line was straight and blended well with his sharp cheekbones. Each cheek displayed a slight dimple below his devilish dark brown eyes.

She, on the other hand, was petite, perhaps five feet and two or three inches. The clothing fit her well, showing off her narrow waste while her dress hung loose and slightly above her well- shaped ankles. Her blond hair was in sharp contrast to his black curls, as her's was quite straight. One could see the curling iron had done its duty causing a slight curl barely above the center of her forehead. Her blue eyes reflected the light in the room from beneath the long eyelashes that protruded from below her carefully plucked brows.

They were a stunning couple, yet while radiating wealth, they were quite down to earth. They spoke of things that everyone was knowledgeable of, even to the roots of their own company and the problems that had been overcome over the years, especially those that Don had helped to contain and sometimes eliminate. The evening continued with each minute a new discussion, another drink of brandy, another glass of wine, or just another cup of *tea in the case of Sam, our once-upon-a- time heavy drinker.*

It was difficult, but I did manage to overhear several different conversations including one that Don and his friend John were having by the fireplace where they quietly picked up on their earlier discussion.

"I didn't mean to stop our conversation just as it was getting started John, but with the guests showing up..."

John understood, "I know, first things first, you have to take care of all of your guests."

"Well, to continue where we left off, this inventory problem is devastating for all of us. I must assume that the panic on Wall Street has stopped several companies in their tracks. As I understand it, even J.P. Morgan, with all of his money, could not stop the thundering herd at the stock market. It fell 50% in November. It was a dreadful thing to happen, especially so close to Christmas."

"Yes, that is true. But just think, if old JP hadn't stepped in, then what?" (1)

Don agreed, "True, that is very true."

Just then, Ward approached them.

"By George, the last time I saw you, you were starting out that new UPS thing. How is it working out?

John smiled as he answered Ward.

"Pretty well, thank you. I am glad you asked because I would certainly like the opportunity to ship your beer to your vendors."

"Really? You know I never thought about that. We use the big trucks, since we have so many stops in one area."

"That may be true, but look at the upkeep on those big trucks, the cost of the drivers, and the problem of getting deliveries made to smaller stores and shops on those narrow streets. Would it not make sense to hire a company that would insure your goods, make regular deliveries in smaller amounts to small shops, and save you money while letting a lot more smaller customers buy from you?"

Don spoke up, "I don't want to interfere with a sales pitch, but maybe you two should set a date when you can talk about this at some length. It might be of value to both of you, don't you agree?"

Ward, with his booming voice agreed and a date and time were set. "By George, you may have something there my boy. Yes sir, you just may have something there all right."

CHAPTER 6

Don walked across the room to his fireplace vantage point. He asked if anyone would like to hear Molly describe her New Year's Eve in New York City. Everyone clapped and found seating. Some of the men leaned against the wall close to where their wives sat.

Molly was embarrassed at being thrust into the center of attention as it was not in her nature to be there. She would just as soon have left the room and let Don do the talking, and she voiced that opinion, though rather quietly.

"Don should not have done this to all of you. I am a terrible speaker," she started.

Ward shouted, and the others followed with a "hear, hear." They all clapped to let her know that they were awaiting her comments.

Embarrassed, she spoke quietly. So quietly in fact that even I had to listen closely to hear every word.

"Well, there isn't much to tell. We took the train from downtown to New York. As I told Margaret," she pointed at her friend, "we were met at the train station by Bill Parsons and his wife Polly, and a very long car called a limousine. To my surprise, inside sat General Dodge of the Union Pacific Railroad, the fellow that your dad," she turned briefly to face Richard Thatcher, "suggested that Don contact on his vacation in Iowa some time ago."

Richard responded, "I wasn't doing much with the company at that time. I believe I was still in college. Isn't that right Don?"

Everyone turned thier attention to Don to hear his answer to Richard's comment.

"Yes, that's true, you were away, in school at the time.

As I recall from previous conversations, no one really knew where Richard was at that time. He was a bit of a scallywag.

Molly continued, "We were assisted into the big motorcar by its driver, who also took us for a ride through their beautiful park, after a brief tour of downtown."

Suzanne interjected, "You mean Central Park?"

"Yes Suzanne, that's right, Central Park. It was so lovely with the wonderful gaslights all through it, on the roadways and on the paths. It was so beautiful at night. I was told that soon the park would have the new electric lights, like the city has recently installed in the downtown."

She was interrupted by a knock on the door. Don made his way to the door and opened it to find his assistant, Rick Weatherby, and his wife, Angela, standing in wait.

"I'm sorry we are so late Mr. Holscomb, my car hit a hole and broke a wheel. By the time I got it replaced I was filthy dirty and had to go back home to..."

"Things like this happen. You don't need to apologize, just come in, and make yourselves at home. Molly is telling everyone about our trip to New York City."

Don took their wraps and ushered his guests into the den. He held up his hand to interrupt Molly.

"Excuse me Molly, I don't know if everyone knows my assistant or not. This is Rick Weatherby, and his lovely wife, Angela. Later you can all get better acquainted."

He turned to his assistant and asked, "In the meantime, and before Molly continues, can I get either of you something to drink?"

"We have interrupted everyone enough Don, but perhaps a hot tea for Angela, to take the chill off, would be in order."

Don poured the tea into one of the cups on the sideboard, handed it to Angela, and returned to his place by the fireplace.

Don turned to Molly, "Please continue hon, sorry for the interruption."

Molly continued, "We arrived at Times Square and there were several wooden risers set up for folks to sit on. We were led to some seats that had cushions on them. The five of us were seated where we could see everything. It was really marvelous," She turned toward her husband, "wasn't it Don?"

Don agreed. "It sure was."

She then proceeded with her description of the midnight dropping of the ball.

"The people were told when it was a minute before midnight, and all of them thronged around the area where we were sitting, and they counted down the seconds; four, three, two, one, and then the fireworks started, the band played and that big ball just seemed to float down to the brick sidewalk. It was so exciting!" (2)

Someone asked, "Was there a loud bang or anything?"

I couldn't see who asked the question, but everyone laughed, and it went unanswered.

"What else did you do Molly?"

Margaret already knew what Molly had done, but thought if she prodded for more information, Molly would divulge more of her experiences to the group.

It worked! She continued on about the ball, the dancing after the midnight drop, the tea at the Waldorf on Saturday, and in general the wonderful time that she had.

All the while, I was concerned that Jim and Claudia did not arrive. Don's brother was always there for every occasion. He would be among the least likely not to come to the gathering.

The evening wore on. More wine was poured and the people mingled with one another, and they talked about this and that, none of which was exciting at all to me.

Finally the guests said their goodbyes with all of the kisses and hugs that went along with the parting. Silence fell over the empty parlor and at last Don and Molly sat down. They appeared to be in an exhausted state.

"I think I am going to have a small brandy to cap off the evening, can I get you anything?"

Molly shook her head no, and Don asked, "It was a fine party, wasn't it hon?"

Molly, with a concerned voice, answered him. "Yes, yes it was, but I am worried since we have not heard from Jim or Claudia, at least by phone. She said they were coming. I hope nothing has happened to them."

Don took a sip of his brandy, and then he shook the ash from his cigar into the fireplace.

"It is strange. It is not like them at all. First thing in the morning we will call and find out if something has happened."

They sat staring at the fire, relaxing for a few minutes before calling the evening finished. Don took the last swallow that finished his brandy. Molly's expression told of her thoughts about her brother-in-law and his family.

Don stood and walked across the room and placed the screen styled spark guard in front of the fireplace, and then hand in hand, they left the room leaving me alone in the den, as they mounted the flight of stairs to their room.

CHAPTER 7

Morning came all too soon. Molly had been up early to prepare their breakfast of eggs, toast, and tea.

"Hurry up Don, breakfast is almost ready. Don't forget, we have an urgent phone call to make."

Don answered sleepily, "I haven't forgotten hon, I just need a moment to shave, and I'll be down."

Molly shouted back up the stairway, "I am very concerned about your brother. It is just not like him to not call."

"I understand that quite well, I had trouble sleeping last night too."

Soon, I heard Don coming down the stairs, two steps at a time. Breakfast was a great enticement to rush, but this morning the phone call was the most important thing on his mind. I waited, with great concern, to hear what could possibly have kept Don's brother from coming. Being a part of this family, for as long I have, it gave me reason to worry too!

Don suggested, "I think we should call right away."

Molly explained, "We will have to have breakfast first or it will be cold. I am as concerned as you, but I don't want to have our breakfast spoiled too." Molly sniffed before continuing, "I should have waited for you before I did this."

"Don't blame yourself for doing what you always have done, if I had any sense I would have gotten up when you did, and made the call while you were fixing breakfast."

Times like these did not come often and for that I am grateful. I have heard of people breaking things, like me, when they were a bit out of control! It was a frightening thought indeed.

Don attempted to soothe Molly's feelings.

"I'm sorry honey. We can't start casting blame on ourselves. A few minutes to eat are not going to change anything. As soon as we get done with breakfast, I will make the call. I'm sure everything is all right, probably just got the dates mixed up. There is no need for you to cry."

I could hear the worry in her voice and a sob as she spoke.

"You always say the right thing. I just feel I should have waited ..., well you know I make breakfast at this time every day, and it's a habit."

Don looked at Molly lovingly as he spoke,

"You are the kindest person in the world Molly. I could not expect more from you than you give. I think that we are both a bit on edge this morning. Please forgive me if I sounded abrupt."

Molly must have smiled, as she answered with a question that really was not a question.

"You know I will, don't you?"

Breakfast was over quickly, and the dishes were put into the sink. Don picked up the receiver and checked to be sure no one was on the line, then I heard him crank the phone for the operator.

"This is Don Holscomb."

Matilda seemed surprised to hear from a fellow who rarely used the phone, and who always sounded like it was a chore to do so.

"Good morning Mr. Holscomb, what number would you like this morning?"

"I would like to call Oakville, Number 18."

Don covered the mouthpiece, "Molly, you can actually hear the number being plugged in. This is a marvelous invention isn't it? The phone is plugged in through the switchboard, and I can hear it ring. I didn't know there were four rings on his end."

"Maybe you don't make enough calls to your brother...suppose?"

Don told Molly that the phone stopped ringing and a strange voice answered.

He removed his hand from the mouthpiece and started talking. I could hear both ends of the conversation as the fellow on the other end shouted into the phone.

"Hello, who is this?" Don asked.

"This is Wayne Hopkins, who is calling?"

"Wayne, this is Don, Jim's brother, is he there?"

"'fraid not."

"What?"

"'fraid he's gone."

"Well if he isn't there, why are you answering his phone?"

"Well, sorry to tell you this. Yesterday he and the family were goin' somewhere and left out of here 'round four o'clock or so, in that jalopy of theirs. As they was makin' the turn down on Bottom Creek Road, a cow came out of nowhere. He turned to miss the darned thing and drove right into that creek."

Don became excited, "Go on man; go on! Was anyone hurt?"

" 'fraid so."

"What do you mean 'fraid so'?"

"Well, that old jalopy turned over and landed upside down in the creek. You know this time of year it's kinda deep, over six feet in some places."

"Go on, go on." Don urged.

"Well... they all got out but..."

"But who? Get on with it!"

By this time I could tell that Don was losing his patience with the man on the other end of the phone. His voice was getting louder and more demanding, and since patience was one of his virtues, I found it strange that he was losing it with this person.

"They all got out but Mr. Jim. He couldn't get away from that steerin' device and by the time they righted that old jalopy, he drowned."

"He drowned?"

Molly had been standing close by the den door next to Don. "Who drowned?"

Don placed his hand over the mouthpiece again. "This fellow just said Jim drowned."

The color drained from Molly's face.

"Jim drowned?"

Don spoke back into the phone with a broken, almost apologetic voice.

"You just said my brother drowned?"

"Sorry to have to tell you that, but that's what I said. Yasser, brother Jim went on to heaven."

"Good Lord, how is the rest of the family?"

"Well, the missus has a broke leg, Mike has a broke arm, and Billy was with a friend, so he wasn't with 'em."

"You tell Claudia that Molly and I will be there as soon as we can."

"And who were you again?"

"Just tell her Jim's brother is coming right away!"

Don hung up the receiver and his breathing seemed urgent. Molly was crying but I didn't understand what was happening even though I could hear quite plainly both ends of the conversation.

This is the second time someone died, and I still don't understand it all, but it must be quite bad. I know that never seeing Kitty or Jake, after they died, has been bad for me and this seems even worse for everyone.

They both rushed up the steps to the bedroom and I could hear both of them removing clothes from the hangers, and dresser drawers slamming, and then I heard a click, click noise.

Molly spoke first, in a quivery voice.

"Did you pack enough for a couple of days? Did you get all of my things in there too? You know you packed and locked that trunk awfully fast."

"Yes I know I did; and yes hon, I got everything we need."

Molly sobbing, told him, "I should tell Margaret we are leaving, I'll do that while you get Lizzie started. I'm just going to leave the dishes soaking; maybe Margaret will come over and finish washing and putting them away."

They both came rushing down the stairs so quickly that I feared for their safety. They dashed down the hall and through the kitchen and then out of the side door at the same time; Molly went to the neighbor's house, and Don to the barn in back where they kept old lizzy. As usual she backfired and Don said a couple of choice words. The door slammed shut at the neighbor's house, the key rattled the lock on Don's, and Molly's side door, and the last thing I heard was ole lizzy backing out of the drive.

The next two days went by slowly. I wondered how Don and Molly were, and if this drowning thing hurt his brother and the family. Then there was the death thing too. I had not seen the boys, Mike and Billy since their last visit in November at Thanksgiving, and could not help but wonder how they were.

A couple of days passed, when ole lizzy came up the drive. She was stopped by the side door to let Molly out, then she continued to the barn. Molly waited at the door for Don, and they came in together. They said nothing, which was very unusual. The joy that always radiated from them was nonexistent.

Sadness prevailed and the gloom of this thing seemed to overtake the house. The fires didn't burn as bright, the smiles and laughter seemed to dissipate and fade away. The happiness, that I had grown so accustomed to, was gone. Don and Molly were sadder now than when Catherine left home. It was almost unbearable, even for me, their clock. The telephone seemed to ring continuously, and flowers came into the house by the dozens. I could not understand what

*was happening any more than I could understand
why Don's brother and family didn't come to visit.*

*I had several conversations with the chair by
the settee, and the table by the big chair Don always
sat in. None of the four of us truly understood what
was happening even though we had been there for so
long and spent many hours trying to understand
humans. This death and drowning thing mystified
the three of us. The more we tried to understand it,
the more lost we became. We could only imagine that
if one of us were to end up as kindling for the
fireplace, perhaps it might be the same.*

*I had difficulty with all that took place for the
next few weeks. Don and Molly spent more time at
Jim's than they did here. I heard, through the
conversations, (all of which were very quiet and
discrete) that Jim had been laid out in his home, and
that folks came from the surrounding area to visit.
Apparently they brought food and desserts and they
brought gifts; they came by car and buggy; and this
continued for a few days. Don and Molly called this
"respect for the family, and saying goodbye to the
departed." I don't understand the saying goodbye to
the departed part, nor did I understand how that all
fit together with drowning or death. It seems to me,
that if one is dead, that has to relate to death. They
can't hear the other humans say much of anything, let
alone goodbye. I have found there are a lot of strange
things humans do that we wood creatures can't
understand, or do.*

Catherine wrote to Molly and Don. It was a sad letter. This is what I could hear so clearly from the den when Molly read to Don across the kitchen table.

Dear Mother and Father,

It is with deep heart that I write this letter, as I loved Uncle Jim so much. I am sure that Aunt Claudia and the boys are going to miss him tremendously as the love in our family is so deep. I can only imagine their grief. Please let them know that could I have come on short notice, I would have, but having to bury Uncle Jim quickly, left little time for me to get there since I would have had many arrangements to make.

Julius sends his regrets, as does the whole family here. They want you to know that should you need anything they will do what you ask, or should you wish to come here to escape the pain of death, you are welcome to do so.

I shall write again soon.

Love,
Catherine

PS: Dad, I know how much you miss Jim and I just want you to know that I love you very much.

Molly burst with sobs after reading the letter. I could hear Don console her, although he wept as well. The time was sad and it hurt me to hear their sadness. The guests that usually came and brought so much cheer and laughter, along with their conversations, still came, but with soberness I had not experienced before.

CHAPTER 8

"Mother!" Billy shouted loudly as he came through the front door. "It isn't true is it, dad is okay isn't he?

A bereaved Claudia, with tears streaming down her sunken cheeks, reached out and took her son into her arms.

She spoke sadly and quietly, "He's gone son, your father's gone."

"How could that happen? He was so careful with his driving, especially with all of us in the car. I don't understand."

"I know, I know," Claudia tried to console him, "he was careful, but that cow came out of nowhere, none of us saw it until it was too late!"

"What damned cow!"

"Mike, you know we don't talk like that in this house." His mother turned her head slightly away from Billy toward her other son.

"I know mother, and I'm sorry but I just can't help it. That cow took father's life and I'm not about to forget it!" He stopped and looked at his brother's broken arm. "Who owns it?"

Billy moved toward Mike and they embraced, as brothers might, in this time of deep hurt and loss. "No one knows, Bill."

The next few days turned into a week, and then two, as Don tried to help settle the family affairs. Claudia wanted to just sell the place and go back to where her folks were; the boys were plotting a way to get rid of the cow, the culprit in their minds. It was a difficult time for all.

There was a gentleman in town that had, at one time, made an offer on the property. At the time, no consideration of selling had entered the minds of either Claudia or Jim. They had been very happy with their place, and they owned it, free and clear, and without any desire to buy another home. Don asked if Claudia did indeed wish to sell out and leave. There were discussions on the pros and cons of the situation, and he asked if he should contact the fellow that had contacted them before.

Claudia tearfully agreed that it would be the thing to do. Don drove to the other side of Oakville and contacted Mr. Sawyer. Fortunately, he was still interested, even though more than a year had passed, and he renewed his offer without even seeing the property again.

When Don asked why he would do that, he explained that he had watched Jim from afar, and he knew how he took care of his home. Consequently, he had no concern about what condition things would be in.

Don, satisfied with the answer, drove the tin lizzy back to his brother's home and told Claudia that Mr. Sawyer would buy the place for $2380.00, same as his previous offer. It was a reasonable price for the place in Oakville, and she readily accepted it. Don proceeded to handle the transaction for her and the deal was consummated within a month. Claudia and her sons were now free to leave for Boston.

Mike and Billy were not as enthusiastic as they could have been. They were both in high school, were on special teams, had many friends, and had never known any other place to live. Claudia assured them that they would make new friends. She told herself that although she had not seen her sister Jenny as often as they had Don and Molly, it had only been due to the miles. Time will heal all things.

Unhappily, the brothers conceded that their mother knew best. They packed their things and said good-bye to their friends. The boys received a special letter of recommendation telling of the efforts they had taken by going to another city to learn the new game called basketball, and then coming back to teach the rules and create a basketball team. They would be sorely missed.

They left town with their mother for their new home. It was discovered shortly after they had left that a certain cow had seemingly disappeared . A strange coincidence!

CHAPTER 9

Although the joy seemed to be gone, guests still came to Don's and Molly's home, the conversations weren't as bright, but time continued to move ahead.

The Eiffel Tower had a radio message sent from it for the first time; (3) a new group was formed called the Boy Scouts and started by some fellow named Robert Baden-Powell (4) (although there were other accounts discussed that a Theodore Roosevelt had a strong hand in it).

Then there was that tin lizzy race that supposedly went from New York to Paris. (5) Of course the question arose about how could anyone in their right mind would try to go across water in a motorcar? That offered some levity, along with laughter, to ease the agony of an otherwise bitter year.

One evening Rick Weatherby stopped by with his wife, Angela.

"Good evening Rick and Angela; come on in. it is good to see you."

"Thank you Mr. Holscomb. Angela and I were just in the neighborhood and thought we would stop by."

Rick removed his jacket, and he gave it to Don to put into the hall closet along with Angela's coat.

"Is there a reason, other than just stopping by, for the visit?" Don asked.

"No, not really, we just felt that we should pop in and be sure you two were all right. It has been two months since your brother's passing and we felt we should stop by and visit for a spell."

"That is very thoughtful of you. Come into my 'den of inequity'."

Don ushered them through the hall and into the den, where they smiled at his name for the den.

"I haven't had my evening brandy yet, and since there is still that chill in the air, perhaps you and Angela would like a glass of wine?"

"That is very nice of you to offer," Rick looked at his wife and asked, "would you like a glass, Angela?"

Angela looked up at Don as she sat down in the chair by the settee.

"That would be very nice. I would love some. It might take the chill off and it sounds better than tea."

Don poured them each a glass of wine, then he filled his brandy snifter a little less than half. He took his old stance by the fireplace, but didn't light his cigar. As a matter of fact, I don't remember him lighting one since his brother's accident.

Rick broke the ice, "Well, what's new in the world Don, anything earthshaking that we should know about?"

"Nothing that spectacular I'm afraid. I was surprised to learn, however, that more oil has been discovered in the Middle East. I understand that the United Kingdom acquired the rights."

Rick's curiosity was aroused. "What do you think that may mean to us, if anything."

"I really don't know at this time, but as I recall, you have always been on top of oil with its storage and so forth. Isn't that correct?"

"It was, but as you will also recall, you decided that should be handled by the maintenance division, and that I should concentrate on learning what I need to know to help you in sales and marketing."

"Oh yes, that's right, I did say that didn't I?"

Don was well aware of what he had suggested, but in a shrewd way, he was attempting to get some information, since he had heard some gossip about the possibility of his being replaced.

He continued, "I might add that it was the right thing to do too. I could not be happier."

Molly had just finished the dinner dishes and came into the parlor. She immediately gave Angela a hug, and then she took Rick's hand and inquired as to their lack of visiting lately.

"We haven't seen much of you since our 'after New Year's' get-together. How have you been?"

Even though she held Rick's hand, the question was directed more at Angela than at Rick.

Angela returned the pleasantry with a question. "Very well, thank you, and you?"

"We are as well as can be expected. It has been a terrible year beginning with the loss and everything, but we will recover, I am sure."

Rick nervously pawed the side of his glass. The beads of sweat from the glass dripped down onto his trouser leg, but he didn't seem to notice. He looked at his wife and then away, toward the fireplace.

Sheepishly he asked, "Don, some of the fellows at work are concerned about you. I have been requested to check in on you and inquire as to your health. There are rumors floating around that you have not been well, and that you are considering retirement. Many at the office are worried."

"In other words, there are those that think I am not capable of handling my work load, is that it?" Don was strangely curt in his question and answer.

"Well, they didn't say that, but yes… sort of. I didn't want to ask you about it, I figured it was someone else's responsibility. I hope you don't think any the less of me for bringing it up?"

Almost belligerently, Don continued, "You know Jim and I were the only ones left in our family, and losing him to something so stupid, as getting killed over a cow, has bothered me!"

"Now Don, don't get excited. You know what the doctor…" Molly paused, but too late.

Don, still in the despair of the moment, "I'm sure these young folks don't want to hear about that."

"I know, I shouldn't have mentioned it."

"Mentioned what?" Rick asked.

"It's nothing!"

Don's face was turning red and his cheeks were puffing. He sat down in the big chair and lit the cigar that he had been holding onto for three months, without lighting. Molly felt forced to expose the truth.

"Rick, Don is under the doctor's care. He has been told to get some rest, and to slow down. He refuses to do it, at least to the pace he should."

It was impossible for young Rick to contain himself. He worshipped the man.

"Dawgone it Don, why didn't you tell someone, I'm sure that they…"

"Sure they would what? The company isn't like it used to be. Everyone used to care about everyone else... but today?"

In an effort to calm his friend and mentor, Rick continued in a quiet voice.

"I think they still do. I know that Angela and I care about you. If I can do anything to lessen the load, I will do it," then he added, "and I don't have to let anyone know about it either!"

Rick finished his glass in one gulp. He asked for a brandy, which was quite unusual since Rick rarely finished a glass of wine. I could only surmise this task was put upon him by someone else, and the pressure was on. Perhaps that glass of brandy will bolster him; he looks like he needs something.

Don took a drag on his cigar, then he apologetically looked at his apprentice.

"I want you to know that you have done a very fine job learning what I do. I could not have asked for a better assistant. Perhaps it is time for me to consider stepping down!"

Rick set his glass on the table beside him; then he shifted in his chair uncomfortably.

"Don, I only meant that perhaps I could take on more responsibility, just until your health is back up to snuff. None of us at the office have any desire to see you step down."

"I know that. Forgive me for the outburst. I just am so upset right now, about so many things, that I don't..."

Rick completed the sentence, "You don't know where to turn. Allow me to tell you that you can turn to us. Neither of us will breathe a word of this conversation." He turned toward Angela, "Will we sweetheart?"

Angela nodded in agreement as she faced Molly, "You know that we are your friends," then she took Molly's hand in her's, "we would never betray you. You are like parents to us."

The young couple had come and delivered their message, then they finished their drink and excused themselves. It was not something that anyone wanted to hear. Don told Molly, after the young couple had left, that maybe it was time to step down.

"This is the first of many conversations like this I'm afraid. After all I am getting up there. I am 53 years old now and soon to be 54. Maybe I am going to have to start thinking about slowing down. You know Jim's death has taken a toll on both of us, and I feel so tired these days. Also, there is the doctor, and what he said. I just have to keep a stiff upper lip."

Molly stared at the fire for several seconds.

"Whatever you decide is all right with me. Now that Jim is gone, and Claudia has moved closer to her own folks, and Jim's boys are both soon to start college; well, maybe it is time for us to consider doing something else... like retirement."

Don suddenly awoke to the reality of what he was saying when he repeated, rather loudly,

"Retirement?"

Molly took his hand in hers, "Yes, retirement!"

"I guess I wasn't thinking about retirement, more about just slowing down a bit! How long have you been thinking about this Molly?"

Molly leaned forward and looked at him, then she confessed, "Since Jim died. You know you haven't been the same, and now of course… there is the doctor."

"Yes, I know, the doctor. What does he know? All I need is a little rest."

"Sweetheart, it has been two months now and you are not any better. I hear you breathing hard in the night, I feel you toss and turn as though you are in agony, and when I ask you about it, you just tell me, you're all right, don't worry, and that you just have a lot on your mind, and then you expect me to just go back to sleep. I love you and I care about you. We don't need this big house any more, you don't need to work anymore. Don, I worry about you."

Don was shocked to hear all of this, especially coming from his, normally so quiet, Molly. She rarely spoke out about much of anything, and he had always been in charge around their home. He was the provider and the protector; to hear her say she thought he was getting weak? This was a blow to his ego, but it was also a reality check, one he could not ignore any longer. His health had been going downhill for some time, his temperament was not as level as it had always been in the past, and his job was becoming more demanding.

"You could be right hon; no," he hesitated, "you are right. I guess I have let things go too far with my feeling so sorry for myself, you know... about losing Jim, and trying to come to grip with Claudia and the nephews leaving. The job has gotten much tougher through the years, and at my age... well maybe I am reaching that point. It would be nice to be closer to Catherine and Julius and little Mable Ann.

Let's sleep on it and then talk about it tomorrow, okay?"

CHAPTER 10

Many things had to fall into place. Don felt he would have to have something to do when they got there, that he couldn't just sit around and do nothing. Then, of course there was the sale of the house, and the purchase of another. Would they want to buy someone else's house, or should they have one built? If they had one built, how long would that take? Should they buy new furniture and sell the present furniture at auction? There were so many details to be handled.

I was content to listen to the discussions, knowing that my thoughts were no value.. Sometimes being an innocent bystander is good, but I was worried that they may leave me behind again, and I would end up in a restaurant, or perhaps even someplace worse.

Being around humans so long I began to worry just like they do. What if someone bought me at auction and then tore me apart? What if some new owner decided to put some unheard of paint color

*over my fine finish? There were so many 'what ifs'
that I was frightening myself just thinking about
them while all the time knowing there was nothing I
could do about it anyway.*

*They might even sell me to Ward and he
would stick me in that smelly old brewery they talked
about so often; or to John Newsome and end up at his
UPS office, whatever that was. Then again, surely
they wouldn't sell me after all of these years,
especially after the difficult time they had getting me
back from Mrs. Dresher and the restaurant, would
they?*

*The weeks turned into months. Henry Ford
introduced the new "Model T" in September. Don
thought that he should buy one so they could drive it
to Iowa. Of course Molly, who rarely argued with
him, suggested that perhaps it would be wiser to take
a train to Council Bluffs, and then buy a new car
when they got there. After all, as she put it, "Eight
Hundred and Fifty Dollars just doesn't grow on
trees," and then she continued on about driving so
many miles with the tire problem they had read about,
and having to buy new ones along the way. Then
there was the lack of service stations; and the length
of time to drive. She won, without a battle, by using
something she called common sense. Don thought it
would be nice to have another of their gatherings and
tell his friends about their plans. Friday,
December19th, seemed appropriate. He would offer
his resignation to The Brass Company, and then
recommend his assistant be promoted and be given a
substantial title.*

It would have to be strong enough to substantiate the influence he would need to fill the position Don was vacating.

Tendering his resignation, in January of 1909, would also give Don the longevity of 30 years that he needed for the meager retirement benefit he was entitled to.

The invitations had to be prepared, the plans made, and all had to fit into the proper scheduling. Margaret would be asked to help Molly with the arrangements. It would be a difficult time for both of them knowing it would be their last party together.

The year of 1907, being what it was, still cast a shadow of financial dread over many people in very prevalent. Don and Molly's home was a bit above the average home on the market and the question was who could afford it?"

A representative came out to look at the place and I watched with fear. I still remembered the last time people came to look at Don's house and furniture. They didn't care about me, or my wooden friends, at all. Certainly they would not engage that nasty Mr. Peabody again, would they?

The representative did not please Don or Molly with the price he thought the property would fetch. He told them that the price for a new, middle class home was only $2,650.00 but that his suggested price was $3,000.00. He told them that he would consider that higher price since it had a tub, had hot water, indoor plumbing, and even had a phone.

I guess that the love and care that had been put into the place, the gatherings that had been there; all of these things had to be laid to the side and not considered. I could not understand how they could do that! Were all of us, the wooden family, just ornaments? Were we just throwaways, something to be admired and then disposed of? What about our feelings? Of course I guess no one realizes that we wooden things have them to..

Don was aghast at the price. He had visions of maybe $3,500.00 or more. They decided to not sign a contract to sell yet, so he told the man he would keep him in mind when the time came.

"Well, I guess we have heard the worst of it haven't we dear?" Don asked Molly.

Sadly, she responded, "I certainly hope so."

She was silent for a moment and then with her "cup half full" nature, she continued.

"Maybe someone we know would want to buy it. They all love to come here, to our parties, don't they?

Don put a damper on her comment.

"I suppose there could be an outside chance for that, but I don't think we should rely on that to happen. They all have fine homes."

"I hope you are wrong, but since you seldom are in these business matters, you probably are not."

Molly busied herself with the grocery list, and the other things she needed to purchase with Don looking over her shoulder.

"I can't believe the cost of things. It is just plain robbery; sugar is four cents a pound, eggs at the outrageous cost of fourteen-cents a dozen. (6) Where will it all stop? Most of our people only make twenty-two cents an hour.
Do you realize that is only $549.12 a year?"

"I know darling. Haven't you realized how lucky we are at our income of almost ten times that much? Now, aren't you glad you received a good education? Aren't you glad our daughter has one, and she can teach, or a lot of other things most young ladies her age can't do? We are indeed fortunate and so is our circle of friends. I can't imagine living on the wages these people make. I think it is quite unfair that we get so much in comparison, don't you?"

Don partially dug his index finger in his cheek, and after giving her comment some consideration , he told her his thoughts.

"Honestly I hadn't given it much thought. We don't run in the same circles as the factory workers do, and they don't run in ours. I guess there hasn't been any real reason for me to think about it. We just pay what the guidelines call for todaywithout really considering the poor workers."

The days flew by and the arrangements were made for that wonderful date in December that I had been waiting for. It looked like joy might return to the place. There was no doubt it was going to be an exciting time for me! The conversations I hoped to hear, and the friends of Don and Molly's, that were surely to arrive all dressed in their finery made it almost impossible to keep my chime quiet.

December 19th arrived and the den was filled with their friends. Everyone was not invited this time since this was a different kind of occasion. It was a celebration that only the closest of friends would be privy to, the closest of confidants, the people that could be trusted with the news they were about to receive.

Don stood with the stance I had become accustomed to seeing before the accident, one hand inside his coat, one foot on the fireplace hearth, and a glass of brandy in his other hand. The cigar was missing since Don had been told by his physician to stop the "filthy habit."

"I am going to start off the evening with a toast. I would like to toast my lovely wife for the many years she has put up with me."

Everyone smiled as they acknowledged his remarks with a smile.

"Next, ,I would like to raise my glass to all of you who have bolstered me in my downtimes, have stood beside both of us in our loss, and have been such loyal friends for these many long years."

Everyone hoisted their glasses and clinked them together as carefully as possible, accepting the toasts and agreeing to their content. They lowered their glasses and took a sip of the Champaign that had been ordered for this very special occasion.

After the toasts had been properly acknowledged, everyone sat their glasses down.

Ward asked, "What is this special occasion?"

Don placed his glass on the mantle, and with a very sober expression asked that everyone sit down. Molly sat on her special settee leaving adequate seating for everyone with the pillows on the hearth, Don's large overstuffed chair, a pair of nicely upholstered chairs that were designed for the dining room, and a couple more sitting room chairs that were also brought in.

After everyone was settled Don answered Ward's question. He reached out, and pulled Molly to his side with his strong arm.

"After months of decision making, we have decided it is time for me to step down as Vice-President of The Brass Company."

Knowing glances were exchanged. Suzanne looked at Sam, Brenda and Ward just smiled as though they had an inkling of what was taking place, John and Shirley just sat as though surprised, and of course Rick and Angela were immediately ill at ease, wondering what was going to become of Rick's job.

Don continued, "I have decided to tender my resignation on the Fifth of January, which is the first Monday of the month. In my letter of resignation I have indicated that the reason is simply that I feel it is time to retire and join my daughter and son-in-law in Iowa and to be a part of our granddaughter's life."

Ward interrupted, "Brenda and I had discussed this very thing just last week. We had a feeling this was going to take place, and on that hunch have brought something to the table. Would you consider staying here and becoming a consultant to our sales force?"

Don was honored with the offer. "Ward, there is no one I would rather be associated with than you and your new brewery, but Molly and I have decided to sell out here, and move to Iowa. There is nothing now that could change our minds, but I do want to thank you old friend, it is indeed a generous offer."

Almost timidly, Rick asked, "Don, will this affect me and my job with the company."

Don winked at Molly without Rick seeing him, "Yes it is! Your job is being eliminated." Rick stuttered, "E...eliminated?"

"That's right, eliminated. Starting on that January date you will be..."

Angela, with a tear welling in her eye, interrupted.

"Terminated?"

Then she held her hand on her chest and gasped.

"No, he will be known as the National Sales Manager."

Rick quickly took his wife's hand as she shed tears of both joy and relief.

"Thank you Don, I don't know what to say except I know you have made this happen."

Don intervened, "No, you have made it happen yourself, through hard work and determination. Everyone is very proud of you."

John spoke up, "There isn't any more news is there? I don't think we could handle it if there was."

"Just one bit more. All trucking of small parts will now be handled through the local UPS office. I guess that is it in a nutshell. We are going to retire and move to Iowa, lock, stock, and barrel."

John's mouth dropped open and he sat silently, as though in shock. He took a sip of his drink and then spoke.

"I don't know what to say, but...well, darn it man, thanks, that's all, just plain, thanks!"

Sam raised his glass and offered a toast of his own. It was short, to the point.

"To the finest folks and friends that a man or woman could ever hope to have, Skoal."

Everyone called out together, "Hear, hear. Skoal."

The brandy was consumed along with a bottle of Champagne, and most of the guests left, unhappy to find that their friends would be leaving, but glad that they would be with their family in Iowa.

Don's assistant Rick, and his wife Angela, stayed a bit longer, still in awe at their new position in life and unable to tear themselves away from their friend and mentor.

The next day arrived quickly. Don and Molly decided that they should write a letter to their wonderful daughter Catherine to suggest that she look into the housing market there. They knew that she would love to have them move to her town as she had voiced it so many times.

A few weeks went by when the knocker sounded on their door. When Don opened it, Rick and his wife, Angela were there standing on the porch. Rick seemed very excited and just blurted out why he was there.

"I don't want to appear too forward Don, but Angela and I have been considering buying a home, when and if I was promoted. Since it appears that has happened, we were hoping that maybe, well…"

He looked at Angela nervously, then back at Don.

"We thought that maybe… oh darn it! Can we buy your house?"

Don was surprised by the request. He had not considered Rick, even though Molly had mused that perhaps one of their acquaintances might be interested in buying the house.

"I suppose you could, but do you think this might be too big a house for you, just the two of you?"

"No. You see we're going to have a baby in another five months or so, we will be parents! You know old folks like…"

Angela nudged him in the ribs.

"Oh there I go again, I didn't mean you were old, or that by being parents you get old," he stuttered again, "I guess I have stuck my foot into my mouth haven't I?"

Don teased, "Well, from one old fogey to another, why not? I have found feet fit well in there." Then he replied to the question. "Yes we would consider it."

"Really, you would really consider it?"

"You know my motto; if you got the money we got the product."

Rick asked, "How much?"

Don answered, "I haven't decided on a price yet, but we have been looking at the market."

"We have too. I have to admit we love your house, and…" He stopped, to be sure there was not a last minute change in Angela's thoughts, then continued, "Would you consider $3400.00, cash?"

Don looked at him in amazement as he replied, "Cash?"

"Yes sir, cash. You see Angela's grandfather passed away last month and left her a tidy endowment. We decided to use it to buy a house if my promotion came through, and it looks like that has happened."

"I see, and what kind of date would you have in mind?"

"Oh we aren't in a big hurry as long as it would be before the baby comes."

Don looked at Molly, who, with a tear in her eye, nodded yes.

Don extended his hand, "Let's shake on it. It is a fine offer and I don't see how we could refuse it. Especially since it would be like keeping the place in the family, kind of."

They shook hands in agreement on the sale of the home, only the date was left unassigned. The deal was done, not foreseeing any problems in the future. The young couple thanked Don profusely and left.

Don looked at Molly in disbelief. "What a stroke of good fortune to have such a wonderful understudy, one that cares so much about our home here, and wants to buy it!"

Finally the letter was written.

Dear Catherine and Julius,

We hope you are well as I write this letter on February 3, 1909. We are well and thinking of you.

I am hopeful that this may come as welcome news, at least that is our hope. Your father and I have sold our beautiful home, here in Waterbury. It is too large for us without you being here with us and since your father has decided to retire this year, the large income to maintain it is no longer coming in either.

If it would please you , we would consider moving to Council Bluffs to be closer to you and baby Mable. Since Jim has passed on and his family have now moved to be closer to your Aunt Claudia's family, we are longing for family.

Please let us know what your thoughts are. In the event this is indeed pleasing news

to you both, perhaps you could send us some information with regard to housing in your city.
Love, as always,
Mother.

CHAPTER 11

February arrived and the long cold month of January at last came to an end. Molly had told Margaret that there were so many things to do that she didn't know where to start, but writing to Catherine had been accomplished telling her that they had decided to move to Iowa.

The house had to be spotless, the coal bin cleaned as well as the basement floors. The canned goods would have to be given away, since transporting them to Iowa would be cumbersome. The car had to be sold.

Don had given his resignation on January the sixth. Of course, as he said several times, this would mean he would no longer be employed, as of March the sixth. He was beside himself with worry that young Rick would not be able to handle the job; then he worried about the company, and how it could possibly function without him. Who would advise the new president, Richard Thatcher?

As for me, there was nothing I could do. Worrying was not something a wooden object does. Wondering yes, but worrying, never, well almost never! There was some concern on my part when I thought about being sold at auction. If I were able to shiver like a human, I am sure that I would, but since I can't, I will just remain reluctant to consider it.

"Chair," I called out to the overstuffed chair sitting by the settee. "Aren't you concerned about the sale of the house?"

At first the overstuffed chair just ignored me as though I wasn't there, but I knew that the wood language of his frame understood me. Just being covered with fine cloth meant little to me, as I had seen those fine cloths both come and go!

I persisted, "Chair, the least you can do is answer me! Let your frame do the talking if you can't do it yourself."

Haughtily the chair, almost with a yawn, answered, "What could you possibly have to say to me?"

"Well, for one thing, you don't have to be so stuffy. I have been around these wonderful people longer than you, or any other furniture in this house. I guess you could say that I am part of the immediate family; and that is more than you can say!"

"Humph, you are not as expensive as I am, nor as important. If it weren't for me, humans would have no place to sit during their long and dreary times spent here in this room."

"Long and dreary," It repeated.

I shouted back, "How inconsiderate of you! Have you not been listening to what they have to say, the exciting things that they do, or all of those wonderful things they tell each other that goes on in the world?"

I had about had it with that overstuffed piece of furniture.

Then the chair spoke up, "As far as I am concerned, it is long and dreary. As to the frame I am stretched over, I cover it for most of its life, so how could it have anything to say?"

It was at that time that a more timid wooden voice spoke, "Mr. Clock, I listen all the time. I feel badly that I can't be out in the open, and see things like you do, and more than that, this overstuffed piece of cloth would not mean much folded up and lying in the corner. If it weren't for me, the chair would not exist."

"Now you listen to me," the piece of cloth spoke up, "I am beautiful! You aren't even finished enough to be exposed, well... except for your legs of course."

The chair was indignant. "Yes, that's true, but my legs are beautifully finished, just like I assume Mr. Clock is. I am important."

I couldn't resist speaking out. That overstuffed piece of furniture was starting to upset me, and being the perfect clock that I am, I felt it necessary to end the argument.

"Let's call a truce. We can all talk quietly and get along if we try. You know before you came along, and before I was sold at auction, I lived in the first home Don and Molly owned. I had friends there, like the kitchen table, and the kitchen chairs. Even the kitchen cabinets spoke occasionally. We never argued, but instead, we discussed things that were important, like the everyday things Don and Molly talked about."

The frame spoke, "I think that would be nice. I can't see anything since I am covered up, and all my legs can see are things close to the floor. It would be nice to have someone describe things to me, sometime."

"Oh all right. I guess I have been a bit stuffy. I'll try to be a better piece of furniture. I just never thought about anything but myself before. The idea of other non-human beings never crossed my satin fabric."

It was then that we started to become friends. I know it was a little late, but since we had so few people stopping by, and now, with the possibility of moving and all, it was just the right time to get things straightened out.

Unfortunately it was just in time for the house to be reshuffled, and probably we will all be sent in different directions, just like last time. Only time will tell.

"Guess what?" Don asked as he entered the side door.

"I have no idea what to guess about. What should I think about?"

"Today is the 10th of the month of February. Another wonderful Tuesday, but do you know what is so special about this particular Tuesday?"

Perplexed, Molly had nothing to say except, "No I don't. But I am sure you are going to tell me."

"You can't guess?"

"Don, you are playing games with me."

I could hear Molly giggle, and that told me she had some idea of what he was about to say. She liked to let on that she didn't know; besides, after all of these years, she was quite aware of his teasing.

"This is a special Tuesday, because in four days, it will be that extra special day when I can spoil my favorite lady."

"You don't mean it is "that day" when you are going to take your secretary to lunch do you?"

Molly put her finger alongside of her cheek as though in thought.

"Oh, that can't be, since it is a Saturday, and you aren't at work. Now let me see, you can't do much with Catherine, since she is far away over in Iowa. I guess that just leaves that terrible little flirt, Shirley Newsome."

"Now Molly, you know that isn't true. Shirley isn't my favorite lady."

Don appeared to be distraught at her answer.

"You don't mean me, do you?"

I could imagine her slinking across the room and throwing her arms around his neck.

"You were teasing me weren't you? With all those other women, there can only be one Valentine in my heart, and that is you Molly."

"I was teasing, and I suppose I should not have, but then we do have some fun don't we?"

Then she changed the direction of the conversation when she asked Don.

"Did you know that a lady, who lived not too far from here in Worchester, Mass., started making the first valentine cards in our country in 1847?"

"No, I didn't know that. I suppose there is a lot more history too?"

"Yes, but none as romantic as how I feel about you."

They came into the den arm in arm. Don turned and faced Molly as he wrapped his arms around her and pulled her close. The kiss he gave her almost made me blush, well that is, if I could blush.

Don looked deep into her eyes, "We have had so many wonderful times in this house; I hate to leave it."

"I do to, but you know, maybe the change will be good for us. Your health has come back quite nicely; a new life is facing us; and, we'll find a new place to live and there will be new people."

"Yes, and that is part of why I hate to leave. Leaving our friends, and having to make new ones, doesn't seem to be fair. I guess we will always have these folks in our hearts but I won't be able to stand in the den with my brandy in hand, and have all of those wonderful conversations, will I?"

Molly felt his insecurity with the retirement and the move and pushed ahead.

"We will have new friends. I am sure that you will find common ground with Julius, and if I remember correctly, he had a friend that you met on the streetcar that you liked too."

Don continued to look into her eyes, "Of course you are right. I was just feeling sorry for myself. We will have family again, and that will be wonderful.

"I was thinking about that car too."

"What car?"

"Remember, we discussed selling old lizzy and getting a new 1909 Model T."

Molly responded, without much enthusiasm, "Vaguely."

"Well, there is a new company out there now. Just opened up, it is called the Hudson."

"That's a strange name for a car isn't it?"

"Well it is being made by the Hudson Motor Car Company in Detroit. I understand it was named after a Joseph L. Hudson, the fellow who opened that Hudson Department Store up there. As I understand it, he put up the money so they had to name it after him." (7)

"That is all very interesting, but why would you change your mind from the idea of a Ford to a new and unproven thing, like a Hudson?"

"It isn't like he is just some fellow off the street who decided to do this. These are strong entrepreneurs, men with vision. I have read that there are eight of them involved, and one was a fellow who was an executive with the Old's group. They plan to make this wonderful car and sell if for less than $1,000.00!"

"The price sounds good, as I recall you told me the new Ford would be more than that, with all the fancy gadgets that come with it."

"The timing should be about right. I don't know how long it will be before we get things settled here and moved to Iowa, but that new car should be available, around July of this year."

With her common sense view, Molly said, "By then, maybe we will be better organized and know what the future holds for us in the new place."

Valentine's Day came and went. Don found a wonderful group of hand-dipped chocolates at the Grieve, Bissett, and Holland Department Store. Molly savored their flavor for days, and was tempted to hide them from Margaret's view; but alas, she could not, and Margaret ate her share as the two of them sat in the kitchen and enjoyed the goodies with their tea. One evening George stopped by, as neighbors often do. He came into the den where we were.

"I guess it won't be long now will it?"

"Not long for what, George?" Don inquired.

George studied his friend's countenance before he spoke.

"To start the big move, of course."

"Yes, it is about that time. March the sixth is my last day. I dislike saying this, but I don't know that I will be ready. It is only a week away, and I hate to think about not having a place to go to work every day."

George looked at him with that twinkle in his eye that he so often had. His rugged face always looked happy, but today it had a different expression..

"I feel badly Don."

Don looked at him questioningly.

"Why?"

"You have had a wonderful life, a lovely wife, and a tremendous daughter that you have every right to be proud of. You have had one of the best jobs around. Now you are going to start a new life, in a new place, meeting new people, seeing new things, and leaving me and Margaret behind. It just doesn't seem right."

"I never knew you felt that way George. You are right about some of that though, I do have the finest family a man could ask for. But then, you have Margaret, your new motor car, a lovely home, and a job that you have held onto as long as we have known each other."

"I suppose," George sighed, "but you know the glass is always cleaner…"

"Yes I know, on the other side. You do realize though, that you have your future right here. It is decided, there are no questions and there are no doubts. There is a lot of peace in the fact that you know where you are, and what tomorrow will bring."

"True, very true, but unfortunately, not exciting."

Don suggested that they have a booster.

"George, let's have a brandy!"

You didn't have to ask George twice. He followed Don into the house and Don poured a little more brandy than usual. It was obvious he thought George needed a bit of bolstering.

"How are you coming with the sale of your house?"

Don took a swallow of his drink, and responded, "Quite well, we haven't told anyone yet, but my protégé is going to buy it. He and his wife made an offer that we couldn't refuse, and in cash too."

George took a sip of his drink, and responded with, "$3400.00 isn't to be sneezed at, that is for sure."

Taken off guard by George's knowledge, Don almost choked.

"I didn't think anyone knew about it yet!"

Again, the "I know" showed in his eyes as George answered his friend and neighbor.

"Don, there are no secrets between your wife and mine, and of course between my wife and me. My lips have been, and will remain, sealed, you can count on it."

The end of February rolled around and retirement was eminent. Even Molly had an itch that couldn't be scratched. Catherine wrote them about a wonderful home, in the block in which they lived, that was for sale by the Christopherson family.

Don sat in his big chair and looked at the picture of the new Hudson Motor Car for a bit. Then he sat forward and looked at Molly. She stopped her knitting when she felt his stare.

"It might be wise to buy a home already built, rather than having to wait for the workers to build one. I am thinking we should consider that Christopherson home that Catherine spoke of, what do you think?"

Molly looked thoughtfully at him.

"I think that could be a wise decision. It is apparently as large as this one; we could rent out a room if need be. It is as modern as our's is, maybe not quite as up to date, but close, and I believe it has some other areas that are even more modern that our's.

According to Catherine, it is a two story like ours, but it has a large front porch, a nice side yard, and a garage. It sounds quite pleasant." Then Molly thoughtfully added, "It also has a new coal furnace and a completely concreted basement, with shelves for my canning, too."

Don leaned forward in his chair and asked, "Do you remember what the asking price was?"

Molly reached into her apron pocket and pulled Catherine's latest letter from it. Don stood up, stretched, and looked down at Molly with a smile.

"Okay dear," Don questioned, "and the price is?"

"Catherine says," Molly ran her finger down the letter until she came to the sentence, "Mother and Dad, it is a bargain at only $2,380.00."

"Sounds good, that will give us more than enough to make the move. How can we go wrong?"

"I don't think that we can." Molly answered.

"Why don't you plan to go out there next week? I'll stay here and wrap up some things like selling the car, having the papers drawn up for our house sale to Rick and Angela, and some other miscellaneous things that need attended to. You can look at the place in Council Bluffs, and make the final decision.
You are the one who will be in it most of the time. I will only be there when I'm not working."

"Don, you won't be working. Remember, you are retired."

"I keep forgetting that, but I will have to find something to keep me occupied. I can't just sit around the house and get dusted, like the clock, can I?"

I felt that comment was an insult. After all, I have been keeping time continuously now, for several years, and never complained once. (not that they could have heard me anyway) Even when they sold me, using that dreadful auctioneer, I remained quiet. I only sit here supposedly doing nothing, because I have no choice. How humiliating! There are times that I wish I could jump up and down, and had arms to wave.

"I've never gone anywhere alone. Do you think I can do that?"

"Of course you can. You couldn't have lived this long with me, and not have been a strong person."

He winked at her before continuing.
"Besides, you will have that handsome new son-in-law of yours to help you if you need any help."

He looked at her with the love that he had always shown and smiled.

"I know you can do anything you set your mind to do."

A smile brightened his face as he turned away from her before continuing.

"Besides, you generally have the final say anyhow."

He turned back again and attempted to pull her close to him, but she lovingly pushed him away, removed herself from his grasp, and gently punched him in the stomach with her finger.

"Have the last say huh?"

She smiled as she left the den to fix dinner.

CHAPTER 13

Don came home from the office on that final day, and described its finality to Molly. I listened as he told her how he walked down the corridor towards his office and the young men whispered to each other. "There he goes. I wonder if I'll be around that long?" and "Boy, he sure is lookin' old, isn't he?"

Molly asked him, "Did you talk to Rick at all?"

Don acted as though he didn't hear her question and continued his account of the last day. I came to the door next to my old office and now it had , embossed on the brass plate, Rick Weatherby, National Sales Manager. I walked through the door and saw Rick sitting at his desk, papers strewn across it, and with a pencil in his hand. I asked him, how it was going, and reached across the desk to shake his hand. He stood up and shook my hand and told me that the place wouldn't be the same without me and that he wished I wasn't leaving.

Hoping to make him feel better about the situation, I told him that it was all right. We all have to leave sometime, and this is my time. I asked if he realized that the average lifespan, for guys like me, is in our late 40's?"

He told me that he didn't know that, but he thought that you and I were exceptional. All of the folks that come to our house are our age, and some even older, consequently he didn't think those statistics really meant much.

He said that he didn't know I started in the factory until today, when someone told him.

I confessed that I did, that there was a fellow who taught me a lot of things I didn't know, and later was responsible for me attending the school that used to be downtown called the Business Academy. I continued telling him that when I returned that same fellow put me in charge of the inventory and told me that someday I would be a vital force in this company, if I kept my nose to the grindstone, and that man was Richard Thatcher Senior.

Molly looked at Don, and with that typical smile that was so perpetually on her face, she told him what she thought.

"You are a kind man, and you have been like a father to him, just as Mr. Thatcher was a father to you."

Don turned and walked out of the den toward the side door quickly, so that Molly could not see the tear that I saw drip down from his cheek. He discreetly disappeared before she could notice. His dignity was intact.

Things seemed to fall into place rather well. As luck would have it, the new UPS office downtown needed another motorcar so Don and John agreed on a price of $400.00. It seemed rather meager at the time, but after all, it was used and simply a means of transportation. The wonderful thing about it was that Don could continue using it until the day he would board the train for Iowa.

I was concerned, more than ever now, about myself, and my furniture friends. No mention had been made about what might become of us.

Molly was leaving on Tuesday, the tenth of March for Council Bluffs. She didn't pack a large trunk, but rather, just a few things she felt she would need for a week or so. I watched through the window as George and Don drove off toward the train station, with Molly in the back seat, and her traveling luggage secured to the rear of the Ford. Margaret, cheeks wet with tears, waved good-bye as they disappeared down the street.

George, even with his gruff exterior, had sadness in his expression when Don and he arrived back home. Having a friend leaving you behind was a difficult time, even for him. Don, with his knack for making things all right, left his neighbor in heightened spirits as he explained how lucky Rick and Angela were going to be to have them as neighbors.

Don felt sad and left his friend in the drive came directly into his den to pour a drink. He was alone now, on that chilly day in March. Molly was gone, the house seemed so empty, and there were so many memories of what had transpired in the old house, the parties, the celebrations, and the birthdays.

He was deep in thought when the door-knocker sounded. Don shouted through the open hallway toward the front of the house.

"Just a moment."

He sat his drink on the table, stood slowly, and left the privacy of his thoughts behind as he made his way through the hallway to open the door, and there, to his surprise, stood Angela.

"Well hello, I didn't expect you. What can I do for you?"

"Two things actually, I came to give you a draft for the house. Rick and I thought you could certainly use it right about now."

She twisted her neck to look past Don and asked.

"Where's Molly?"

"Molly just left for Iowa a few minutes ago. I thought you knew that she was leaving today." Don chuckled. "This wasn't necessary. We would not have starved."

Angela sounded embarrassed that she didn't know the time of Molly's departure.

"I guess I thought it was later that she was leaving, but that is all right. Would you consider selling us the furniture, too."

"Yes, we would consider that, but why? Don't you have your own furnishings?"

Don sounded stunned at her request.

"You see, while Rick was learning the business, we have been living with my parents. It was a necessary arrangement, since we were just getting started in our married life. Of course now, that is no longer necessary, with the promotion and all," she stuttered slightly, then blurted out, "but we would have to be finding suitable furniture for your..." she changed the ownership of the house, " well soon, our lovely home."

"I see. Would you want it all?"

Angela smiled, and then she replied, "Yes, all but the clock."

"All but the clock?" Don sounded surprised.

"Yes. Molly has told me so many times about the way you bought the clock, twice in fact, and how much she loves it. I wouldn't dream of even trying to buy the clock knowing that."

"And the rest?" Don asked.

"Everything else fits perfectly. You and Molly have such great taste. I am sure you will want to have furniture that fits your new home… when you get it. It would be a shame for you to have this all go to an auction, or something like that. Would $350.00 be reasonable?"

I don't know if Don heard that or not, but I did.

"Hey chair, did you hear that?"

I have to tell you that if I could cry, I think I would right about now.

"Can you believe what we all just heard?" I am so relieved, and to think I have been worried all this time, if I could worry, that is.

The chair didn't reply. Maybe it feared that humans could hear us, but that didn't matter to me. I was just happy to know that I would be going with Don and Molly, and that the house would continue on with all of my furniture friends that made it a home for everyone who came to visit. It was wonderful to know that the young couple moving here loved everything so.

Don was relieved as he took her draft. Now every detail had fallen into place and he and Molly were free to move to Iowa.

Imagine, in just a few days the car had been sold, the check for the house was in his hand, and now the furniture was sold, and for $350.00 too.

I overheard that long distance calling was relatively new, and very expensive on the phone system. It surprised me when Don raised the phone from its hanger on the side, turned the crank a couple of times, and then shouted into the thing.

"Hello Matilda, are you there?"

I could hear her shouting back.

"Of course Mr. Holscomb, I'm always here, who can I ring up for you?"

"I want to call out of town."

"You mean long distance?"

"If that's what they call calling out of town, yes."

"Okay, where to?"

"Council Bluffs, Iowa."

"Where?"

"Council Bluffs, Iowa."

"Can you spell that for me?"

Don looked like he could jump through the phone and strangle poor Matilda, but he settled down, the redness left his cheeks, and he carefully spelled it out.

"That would be, C-o-u-n-c-i-l -B-l- u-f -f –s- I-"

"Okay Mr. Holscomb, I can handle the Iowa bit. Should I spell this back to you, just to be sure?"

"For goodness sake no, just get me to the operator."

"Don't be too hasty Mr. Holscomb, I can only do this so fast. I have to make the proper connections. Not to be nosy, but I heard you quit your job and are leaving town, is that right?"

"Matilda, I do consider that being nosy!"

"I know, I'm sorry, just wondering."

A new voice came through the receiver, "This is your Des Moines operator in Iowa, can I help you?"

"I didn't want Des Moines, I wanted Council Bluffs."

"I'm sorry sir, but we don't have lines running into Council Bluffs at this time."

"What good is this phone then? I have an important call to place."

"I'm sorry sir; you will have to send a wire to that location."

"A wire?"

"Yes sir, a wire. Can I give you that number?"

Totally confused now, Don answered, "No, it probably wouldn't do me any good since I'm calling from Connecticut."

"I'm sorry sir; did you say you wanted to call Connecticut?"

I don't ever remember seeing Don so flustered. He almost broke the phone slamming it down on the receiver hook and then he just stood in the doorway staring at the floor. His face was bright red, his hair almost on end, his eyes were bulging and it looked as though he were about to explode.

He stormed through the door, walked over to his corner stand beside the fireplace, leaned down, and took a cigar from the humidor. Then he pulled a long fireplace lighter match from its container, struck it on the side of the fireplace's inner wall, lit the cigar and just stood there puffing. I imagined that a steam engine would look the same way, according the descriptions I had heard.

I felt sorry for him, but there was nothing I could do. I suddenly realized that it was three o'clock. My chimes moved into motion marking the hour. It was the first time I ever heard Don tell me to "shut up!"

A few more days passed, and the phone rang the two rings that denoted our phone's identity on the party line.

Don answered it, but not willingly.
"Hello!"

Apparently it was a weak connection and there was static on the line. I could barely hear what was being said on the other end of the line, but I could hear Don, as he held up his end of the conversation.

"Yes, yes this is Don Holscomb. What? I can barely hear you"…Yes, I will accept the charges …pause… "Hello, is that you Molly? It is so…what?"... pause… "You did what?"... pause… "Can you speak louder? Yes, that's a little better but still pretty weak. I didn't understand, did you say something about the house? Can you talk louder?" …pause… "Calling from where? Omaha?

Okay, that's better, now what were
you saying about the house? You bought it?
How soon can we?" ... pause... "You said what?
Next week? You want to stay there and I can
come later this week, is that what you said?"

*Between the expression on his face and the one
sided conversation that I could hear, it was clear that
Molly had purchased the house that they had heard
about from Catherine, and she wanted him to come
there for something, this week.*

"I will repeat to you dear; let me know if
this is correct, okay? ..pause...Okay, you want
me to come there to sign the papers because you
bought the house?" ...pause... "Yes, yes I
understand. Yes, I did sell the automobile. John
bought it for his UPS office. What? The furniture
won't fit? That's okay, I sold it"... pause... "I
said I sold it and no, of course I didn't sell the
clock!" ... pause ... "Okay, okay, I'll catch the
train on the 13th".... Pause ... "No, the 13th.
That will be tomorrow"...Pause... "Okay, see
you then. Bye Hon."

*I didn't know whether to be pleased he didn't
sell me and that Molly wanted me, or to be unhappy
that I was going to be left alone again, and not
knowing for how long. I didn't even know if I would
be wound while he was gone since Molly wasn't here
to ask Margaret from next door to wind me.*

CHAPTER 14

It is Thursday night already, and Don will be leaving tomorrow morning. George just stopped by and is having one last brandy with him. Even though I listen intently, I can't comprehend what they are talking about because I am too nervous.

"George, I am leaving tomorrow. I guess we have bought a home in Council Bluffs, Iowa; at least that is what I got from the conversation I had with Molly on the phone."

"Have they got the lines going all that way now?"

Don answered, "Well, yes and no. They just skipped right over Council Bluffs and the Missouri River and into that other place across the river. Why I don't know, I hear that it isn't much of a place, that Omaha. It's even in another state."

George inserted, "The important thing, I guess, is that you got the message."

Don stopped and looked at the floor.

"Maybe, but you know sometimes I still wish we weren't moving, but I guess it's too late now. Are you going to be around on Friday?"

George's face contorted, and his lips formed a vague, yet ubiquitous smile.

"As often as you need me, I'll be around. I have made arrangements with my boss to let me off work, as needed, to help out here. He is friends with your Mr. Thatcher's family, and that helps."

"You don't need to go out of your way George, you know I can take the streetcar, if need be."

George smiled, "Not on my watch! Besides, if I didn't take you, and Margaret found out… well I wouldn't have a minute's peace without Molly here to settle her down. You should know how she feels about you folks. I know if the shoe were on the other foot…"

"Point made, my friend."

The rest of the evening was spent packing Molly's remaining clothing, Don's wardrobe and unfortunately, me. How I hated that slatted crate and the excelsior that was supposed to keep me from damage while being wrapped in a sheet. All in all though I decided it was best for me to be happy that I was going to move with Don and Molly rather than stay behind once again, as I had done so many years before. I wonder where they kept that crate and excelsior all of these years?

Friday morning came, and the hour for Don to leave approached quickly. George stuck his head in the doorway and asked if Don was ready, since it was already going on eleven, and the train was to leave at precisely two-thirty in the afternoon, railroad time.

"Yes, I'm almost ready George. I'm just putting on my tie."

"Can I fetch your bag or something?"

"Thank you George, it will take the two of us to get this trunk down the stairs."

As George topped the stairs, he was met with Don's remark.

"We men are happy with less! It is indeed fortunate that we have something to pack all of Molly's belongings in, plus the few of my own. I am thankful to have a substantial trunk. Between my few belongings, and the rest of Molly's, I could barely pack safely."

George, answered, "Come on now, we don't want to be late."

I could hear them heaving and panting as they struggled down the stairway, jockeying that large trunk so filled with their belongings. This was one of those times that I wished I was a human and could lend a hand, but I guess I will be captive to this mantle instead and just offer my best ticking.

The clothing and memorabilia packed, the clock secured, all the readiness had come to fruition. I could only ride along and keep best thoughts of a safe journey in mind. I was pleased to be in route to my new home.

George drove, with Don riding beside him rambling on about the fact that soon he would be in a new town, have new people around him, and be out of work. That last part, "being out of work" was indeed depressing he thought. It would be even more depressing if it weren't for the fact that he would be close to his wonderful wife, their daughter and her husband, as well as that four-year old granddaughter of his. She, herself, was a Godsend.

CHAPTER 15

"I am so glad to see you Molly." Don threw his arms around her joyously, "the train ride seemed to last forever, it's as if we have been separated for months rather than just a week."

From my vantage point on the rail car I could look through the small opening of my packing and see Don stop and view his new surroundings, and then he looked down.

"And who do we have here? This can't be Mable Ann now, can it?"

He looked lovingly at little Mable standing in front of him. Then he raised his gaze, "And you Catherine, you are so beautiful, just like your mother."

Molly stood by silently, as Catherine spoke.

"Father, it is so good to see you. It has been some time. "

She stood back and looked at him admiringly, "You haven't changed a bit."

Don answered, "You and your mother must have gone to the same school of compliments. Of course you have to say nice things to me, but I fear that such compliments may cease after I've been here a while."

Molly interrupted and made a suggestion.

"Why don't you pick up your little granddaughter? She has been very patient, waiting for you to give her a hug?"

Don leaned down and picked up little Mable Ann in his arms and then he kissed her on the cheek. "And how is my little lady today?"

Timidly, Mable Ann answered, "Quite well, grandfather, thank you."

The answer was totally unexpected, Don was so taken back by her answer that he appeared to be dumb for a moment or two.

When he awoke from his momentary trance he asked, "You are a clever little one, aren't you?"

Before he or anyone else could say anything, Mable Ann replied in her innocence, "My mother told me to say that. She has been having me practice saying it all week."

Don smiled as he spoke, "Out of the mouth of babes the truth will come. That is what I was always told, and now I know that it is the truth."

Don and Molly laughed as poor Catherine just stood by speechless. She was too embarrassed at her daughter's little speech to say a word.

Molly broke the silence. "Mable Ann, you are going to have to lead us home. Do you remember how to get there?"

"Yes grandmother."

Don looked at his daughter.

"What a wonderful child. You have done an excellent job raising her…so far."

The conductor removed all of the baggage from the train and set it beside the baggage car. Don looked over the assorted bags and found the trunk and his valise, but he missed me.

"Can I carry it for you grandfather?" Mable asked.

The valise was much too heavy for a little girl the size of a jellybean.

"I'll tell you how you can help me. You be sure that Grandmother Molly gets to your house, and I will see to this big trunk, okay?"

Molly arrived safely at Catherine's well ahead of Don. When he got there, she intercepted him and told him how Julius came out of the front door to meet them, and that the first question was about his hereabouts. She told him how Catherine had explained that he had to hire transportation for the trunk and me. Don walked from around the wagon, where Molly had caught him, and there was his son-in-law.

"Hello father Holscomb, it is good to see you. Did you have a nice trip on the train?"

Don extended his right hand and shook hands with his son-in-law. It was good to see the handsome face, with its reddish-brown lock of hair laid neatly just above his son-in-law's forehead.

Julius didn't look like he did the last time Don saw him. His long sleeves were held in place, just above the elbow, by a garter on each arm, he was wearing glasses, which he had not worn before. The top button of his collarless shirt was buttoned but he wore no tie. His trousers were those of a workman. They were clean and pressed, and that indicated that he was through with his work for the day.

"Yes, it was long and boring, especially the stop in Chicago and a few other places. Each extra stop meant time away from my getting here to be with all of you, but that was to be expected," Don paused, then asked, "how have you been?"

"I have been very busy. The carpenter trade has kept me going quite strongly as of late. There are several new houses being built across the street, as of course, you can see, and I am helping there."

Don turned, and looked across the street.

"I can see that you have indeed been busy."

Catherine spoke up, "He has been being sure that everything in the house that you are buying is perfect too!"

"Now Catherine," Julius scolded, "didn't we decide not to say anything about that?"

"I know we did, but I wanted father to know that you have been trying to make their home perfect," then she turned to her father, "and I dare say without the usual delays one has to put up with in this construction trade."

Molly, who had been holding onto little Mable, looked fondly at her son-in-law and daughter.

"Isn't it wonderful to have your father here now?"

Then she walked up the steps and onto the porch beside Don and kissed him on the cheek. The rest of the evening was spent catching up on the latest news about the economy, the city problems, and what was being done and not being done. There was no brandy available, but Julius did have some ale on hand for the celebration of Don's arrival and it quenched his dry and dusty throat.

"Julius, you have a fine home here, it is a fine tribute to your trade.

Don lifted his glass in a make believe toast to his son-in-law.

"May your life be long and your health be good."

Julius replied "Skoal."

They drank their ale, and after doing so, they got up from their chairs. Julius took the valise, and he escorted Don to his in-law's room.

After they had left the room, Catherine looked lovingly at her mother's face. "I think they are going to get along well, don't you Mother?"

Molly smiled, as she always did when she was pleased.

"Yes I am sure they will. How could they not?"

The morning came early and at long last I was taken out of my crate and placed on the dresser.. Don and Molly slipped out of their bedclothes, and Don carefully splashed water on his face from the large bowl beside the bed. It was refreshing and helped his eyes to open after the dust of the previous day. Molly followed suit, although less vigorously.

"Are you ready to see your new home?"

"Yes, I am so anxious to see it that I probably won't be able to eat breakfast."

"To save you all of that agony," Molly pushed her finger against his waist, "take a look out of this window."

Don walked to the window, and he was astonished to find his new home so close by. He had not realized it would be next door, but he was indeed very pleased that it was.

"How great! I won't have far to go to visit our granddaughter, will I?"

Molly responded, "No you won't, and neither will I."

Together, as newlyweds might, they walked hand in hand down the stairs, through the hall and into the kitchen.

"Good morning," Catherine cheerfully greeted them as they entered the kitchen, "I hope you had a pleasant night?"

Don answered, "We did, slept like a rock, except for the train whistles."

She joked back in her unique way, "I guess I should have warned you about that. We are so used to it that we just don't hear them anymore." Then she added, "Of course you must remember it is your friend, General Dodge that is responsible for those whistles." (8)

Don laughed, "I guess that would be right."

It was more like a feast than a breakfast. Catherine has been in this farm type community long enough to prepare a fine meal. She asked Don if he could eat two eggs, over easy, four slices of freshly cut ham, fried potatoes, toast with homemade preserves and a newer thing, at least for Don, coffee.

Don answered in the affirmative, then he made a strategic error, and rectified it carefully.

"You know what?" *Before anyone could answer, he continued,*

"This is without doubt the finest breakfast I have ever been offered."

He offered a brief explanation. "Excuse me Molly, except for yours of course."

The mistake made, he felt he may as well continue, even if not the wisest of things he had decided..

"I will probably walk over here every morning instead of making your mother toil over the stove!"

"Now Don," Molly scolded.

"I know, I know. I probably went overboard, but you know you have taught your daughter well. What a cook!"

Catherine blushed since her father had caught her completely off guard and she was not prepared for such praise.

"Thanks dad. I am glad you are enjoying your breakfast."

Then she turned to her mother and joked.

"I guess you didn't tell him we have only one meal a day, did you?"

Don looked at her with surprise, as did Molly, then they both erupted in laughter when caught the gist of the joke. Only Catherine, with her quick wit, could have pulled that off so easily, and without earlier contemplation.

There was a knock at the front door and Catherine walked by the parlor door to answer it. Don and Molly heard an excited sounding voice as it echoed through the hall.

"Hello Catherine, has he arrived yet?"

"Yes he has Sam, and I know he would love to see you. Would you care for some coffee?"

Sam followed Catherine into the kitchen where Don was finishing his first cup. Catherine discovered that Molly had already started washing the breakfast dishes.

"Do you realize how long it has been since we have done this together?" Molly inquired.

Catherine picking up a dishtowel, responded, "It has been some time that is for sure."

Don stood and shook hands with Sam. "It is good to see you. Our last meeting was quite brief and accidental."

Sam smiled, "Yes it was, but the minute we spoke I felt something special, and then to find you were my best friend's father-in-law...well that was almost too much. I am sure glad you have decided to move here, it is just top notch!"

Don sat back in his chair, "We are glad to be moving here too. It seems like a splendid place to relocate, especially since Julius, Catherine, and little Mable Ann live here."

Catherine turned and faced Sam, "I'm afraid Julius isn't home, he's down at the jail.

"Jail?" Don exclaimed in disbelief.

Catherine, seeing his concern, answered quickly, "Didn't I tell you that he does janitorial work there, and at the city hall? I thought that I had told you that before."

"Now that you mention it, I do vaguely remember that. You know we have been so busy since you were there, it was over four years ago now that the wedding took place...it was undoubtedly in one of your letters."

Catherine interjected, "In other words father, you just forgot."

Don smiled an abashed smile, and knew that he was caught, "Yes, I guess, as much as I hate to admit it, I did forget."

Sam finished his coffee and addressed Don, "Sir, I hope that we see each other again soon. I have to get to work now, but it has been top notch to see you again."

He donned his cap, shook hands with Don and left the kitchen.

"Nice young chap, that Sam Nielsen. He certainly loves that "top notch" business. I think it is good that you two have such a friend. It is easy to see that you get along quite well."

"You're right daddy, we are lucky to have him as a friend, although from time to time I tend to see way too much of him and his "top notch" phrase."

"Well honey, good friends are hard to come by. We may get tired of seeing them from time to time, but later on you will discover that you may never see them again, and that is when they become more precious to you than ever before."

Catherine caught an air of loss in her father's voice. "You aren't talking about the folks you left behind, are you father?"

"I guess I am sweetheart. Time goes by so quickly, that when you leave never to return, you regret your lack of caring, and then you realize that you could never have had them around too much."

Molly looked at both of them, "You too always seem to come to an understanding, whether the conversation is trivial or deep. We are lucky aren't we?"

Don stood and put his arms around them both.

"We are indeed lucky. Now, how about looking at that house we just bought? We have papers to sign to make it all legal?"

Molly and Catherine both removed their aprons. The three of them left through the back door of the kitchen and the porch.

Don took a few steps toward the place, then he stopped. "It looks empty."

"It is empty daddy. The Christophersons have moved to their new place already, in Omaha. Why they are going there I will never understand. It is difficult for me to comprehend why anyone would want to live over there with that cattle stench and the "wild west" atmosphere."

Don asked, "But then, if they had not moved, where would we be?"

Molly answered, "Nowhere probably. We would be making pests of ourselves while a new place was being built."

"Mother, what an awful thing to say, you and daddy could never be pests!"

As they approached the back door, Don turned and said nonchalantly, "Yes we could."

Catherine opened the door and her parents followed. Don could see that the back porch was adequate and would accommodate a nice rocking chair or two, plus a small table. It was screened in and could be perfect for sitting with a cup of tea, or coffee, and relaxing while reading the paper.

The kitchen entrance was through the inside porch door. It was a lovely large room with an empty space for a table and four chairs. Around the perimeter of the room were cabinets with newer appliances. The stove was one of the newer models with Nickel doorframes and front legs, a Nickel Victoria trivet adorned the rear of the splash panel. On the left side, there was a compartment for pans and other baking utensils. The rest of the front was a door that covered the huge oven. The four burners on the top each had a cover, so when not in use one could set things on them. The black cast iron had metal facings made of Nickel that made the stove an elegant piece for the kitchen. Of course it was gas, the newest and most modern thing.

The opposite and outside wall was outfitted with a very large white sink. Above it, two faucets handily protruded from the wall, both adorned with White Ceramic handles, one marked with an "H" and the other with a "C." There were no chips and the drain strainer looked to be new.

Next to the sink they had installed an icebox. It was quite deluxe with its "French Door" affect. The upper left hand door was for ice storage and also had a small compartment over the ice chest for those things that should be kept frozen overnight. The lower left door covered a metal-coated compartment that had a hole in the middle of its slanted floor with a hose attached to it to allow for the melting ice to drain into it, and drip through the porch floor. The right top door, the largest of the four, was for the storage of foodstuffs that must be kept cold, while the bottom right hand door was for condiments.

Molly was overjoyed at the kitchen and content to stay there without seeing the rest of the place. She loved the abundance of counter top space and cabinets.

Since the signing at the barrister's office was just hours away, Don suggested they should move on.

There was a short hall that led to the parlor; on the right hand side was the dining room which could easily accommodate the family. A table and eight chairs would fit nicely leaving ample space for the breakfront and buffet. On the left was what could be a bedroom, or perhaps a den. Taking a few more steps and moving to the left, they found a parlor with room for two large couches, two overstuffed chairs, and a settee and all could be placed facing the fireplace.

The front entrance was beside the stairs that led to the second floor and across the hall from the parlor.

Don looked at Molly and told her he was very pleased with her selection, then he asked, "Where is the bathroom?"

Molly looked back at him and replied, "Upstairs silly, where it ought to be." She pointed to the stairway beside the front entrance. "There, up those stairs."

He made his way up the stairs and discovered a nice bathroom and three nice sized bedrooms. One was at the end of the hallway and would be perfect for him and Molly.

That afternoon they became the new owners of the Christopherson house.

CHAPTER 16

The first of May came quickly and Don and Molly found themselves in their new home at 1518 South 8th Street, in Council Bluffs, Iowa. For me it was exciting. I was glad to see Catherine again and hear her laughter. To be a part of Don's family, without fear that I would be eliminated as a mere piece of furniture, gave me uplifted spirits. As I reflect back on the days of the auction, so long ago, I feel relief to know those days will never be a part of my life again.

The hearth is smaller than the one in Waterbury and, of course, the mantle is therefore equally as small. I really don't need a lot of space, but it did take some getting used to. I realize I could not stretch out my arms... but after all, even wood has to breath.

I have no idea how days move so quickly, but June came overnight! It was such a busy month, and it would have been nice to spread some of those special times around. My birthday was insignificant, and consequently no one but I, was even cognizant of it.

I still recall that day when they put the finishing touches on my, and old Rosie's, wooden bodies, and the day they inserted those awful looking works inside. The finale of it all was when that beautiful pendulum was added. That was on June 3, 1879.

There were really much more important dates to commemorate, such as June 2, Don's birthday. I calculated that this year he would be fifty-five. Then there is Catherine and Julius's wedding anniversary, June 6. It gives me great pride to think about the fact they have been married nine long years. Then last, but most certainly not least, my Molly will be 54 years old on June the 14th. I have been so fortunate to have been with them since shortly after they were married and moved into their lovely house in 1879. I have been with them thirty-one years now and the time has flown.(Well that is, if time can fly!)

"Molly," Don called down from their bedroom, "is this Thursday or Friday?"

Molly was in a cheerful mood, and it reflected not only in her voice, but also in her teasing.

"It is Thursday! For goodness sake are you becoming that forgetful?"

"I don't know. It seems like since I retired, and we have moved here, time works differently. I have so much time to do everything that I don't get anything done; then the day is gone and another takes its place. I just can't seem to keep up any more."

Molly took a deep breath as she continued to prepare breakfast. She knew that Don was right, that time seemed to have no meaning since they had retired. There was no office for Don to rush off to, no meetings, and no traveling from one place to another. They had not even had a party like the ones they used to have. Maybe what they needed was a party.

No sooner had the thought struck my pendulum than Molly voiced it!

"Let's have a party. I know we don't know many folks here other than Julius, his brother with his wife, Anna Jepsen and maybe her brother-in-law Val and his wife, but we could include young Sam too."

Don agreed, "That sounds like a great idea. We used to have such great conversations, and laugh and create wonderful evenings. When shall we do it."

"What do you think about..." Molly paused in thought, then continued her question, "about July 4th?"

"I think that would be wonderful. That is the day of the big fight too."

"Fight? What fight?"

Don looked at Molly as if she should have known.

"Black Jack Johnson and James Jeffries, that's what fight, I can't imagine you not knowing that!"

Molly smiled, and followed Don into the parlor and sarcastically continued with her end of the conversation.

"Oh my, how could I have forgotten, that is so important."

Don, recognizing things were not going well, tempered his questioning somewhat.

"But Molly, the newspapers have been full of news about this fight."

"I have had better things to look at than news about some overgrown boy beating up on another one. Thank goodness you were never a fighter."

Don continued the advertisement, "This colored fellow is six feet and five inches tall and weighs well over 200 pounds. Can you imagine how big that is?" (9)

"No, and I really don't care. I am just glad I don't have to sew up his clothes."

"Come on Molly, be serious. They are going to telegraph the news about this fight all over the country from Reno, Nevada. There are even those that think it is terrible that a black man gets to enter this gentleman's game."

Molly disgustedly replied, "Gentleman's game my foot! What is gentlemanly about beating someone senseless? It is ridiculous, that's what I call it."

"Well there are those that would disagree with you. He is only the second black fellow to challenge someone in the ring, and old Jeffries is coming out of retirement to prove he is still the best fighter."

"Boys will be boys. We will have the party on that night and I would wager not one person will give a second thought to this fight."

"Time will tell. I still think it is a good time for a party, being the 4th of July and all."

Molly rang the final bell suggesting that Don check into his patriotism.

"Could be, but I think remembering what the 4th is all about would be a better reason for the party."

Don was embarrassed, and recognized that he had been out maneuvered.

"Of course you are right. Our independence is much more important than this fight. I'm sorry for making such a big deal out of the fight."

He kissed her on the cheek and left the parlor feeling quite badly. I have seen that look before and I know that Molly has won this debate, at least for now. This fight business was a mystery to me. Only my imagination could help me, and one has to have some experiences to have imagination.

My only experiences were based on what I heard back in Waterbury and what little I have heard here since the move. As I recall the closest thing to beating someone up might have been when Mr. Peabody came to the restaurant and Miss Jenny had that strange piece of wood in her hand. I guess I will just have to wait for more of an explanation on the 4th.

Molly walked next-door and asked Catherine if she would consider stopping by to discuss the party. She apparently obliged her mother as she was at the door just minutes after Molly returned.

As Catherine entered the kitchen door, Molly started bombarding her with questions about the guest list.

"I think your friend Sam would like to come, don't you"?

Catherine responded as she closed the door behind her.

"There is no doubt about it mother, and I think you should ask his fiancée too."

"Fiancée? I didn't know he had one."

"It isn't general knowledge yet, and he hasn't said much about it, but Kathleen told me about it the other day."

"Really? And who is this 'Kathy'? I would love to meet her.

She corrected her mother before answering her question. "No mother, it is not Kathy, she prefers Kathleen." Then she continued, "It's hard to tell. They have been 'off and on' for a couple of years now."

You see she is a Catholic girl, and he is a Nazarene boy. It is almost forbidden for one to change to the other's beliefs."

Molly put her note pad down on the side table. I could see she was going to say something she thought was important.

"It is such a shame that we have to segregate people by religion or faith. I have no idea what the different religions have to do with individuals. After all, it isn't as though one was Jewish and the other an Irish Catholic."

Molly bit her tongue after she said it. Was it possible that she too was a segregationist and didn't know it?

Catherine wisely passed over her mother's comment.

"Mother, you are right, it is a shame. They are both such wonderful friends of ours. We never entered into conversations about their differences because it never seemed important, until he asked her to marry him."

Molly picked up her pad. "If we are going to invite them both, why not invite their parents as well?"

"Mother, I don't know if that would be wise or not. Having them all, at this time, might aggravate the situation to a point that it could get completely out of control."

Molly put her pad back down.

"How could things be any worse if the poor dears are afraid to get married? I know how concerned I was about your Julius, but I don't recall thinking about religion at the time. Parents do worry and try to keep their children from unneeded pain, but..."

Catherine interrupted, "But Mother, if you had tried to keep us apart, we would have found a way, I am sure of it. I think that Sam and Kathleen will find a way."

"Perhaps you are right. I won't invite them, maybe another time, when we get to know Sam and Kathleen better. It would be no surprise for me to find myself sitting in this very room and witnessing a great discussion on religious backgrounds in the future with both of Kathleen Osbourn's and Sam Nielsen's parents."

"I am glad you decided to not pursue this Mother. It is for the best, I am sure."

Mother and daughter once more set about the task of party guest preparation. They agreed that having this nice parlor to sit in, for things like this, was rather nice.

Don had taken over the little room close to the kitchen in their new home. It was there that he did his letter writing, paying the bills, and other things that the man of the house was supposed to handle. It was there that he was allowed his awful smelling cigar, that is of course, if he cracked the window a bit to let the smoke and lingering odor escape.

CHAPTER 17

The 4th was going to be exciting. For the first time I was going to see young Sam and his fiancée Kathleen. Although I have seen the relatives before, it was some time ago and it was at the wedding which was a confusing turmoil. I couldn't help but wonder if Anna Jepsen ever smiled, or if Val's wife ever stopped complaining. It was going to be interesting.

"This is the first time in the last several years that I won't have Margaret helping me. I feel as though I have lost my right arm."

Don put his arm around Molly, and as he did so, his smile broadened, "But now you have our very own daughter to help, don't you? Remember when you and she used to do a lot of these things together?"

Molly looked thoughtfully at him, "Of course I remember. But it seems that Margaret was always there too, even then."

"Have you written her since we have been here?" Don inquired.

"Yes, once, right after we got here I wrote, and told her we were all right and I described the new house, especially the kitchen."

"So admittedly you have only written once in, let's see now…almost three months?"

Molly was embarrassed when Don reminded her that she had only written to her friend once since arriving in Council Bluffs.

"And how long since you wrote to your men friends?"

"That's another story."

Molly, feeling the need to retaliate, asked, "Another story huh? You are chiding me over one person I didn't write to, and yet you haven't written to any of the fellows?"

It was his turn to be qurried, and he knew it; but after all, as I understand these human beings, a lot more of the responsibility for the home falls on the women while the responsibility of the bills, savings, repairs, and outside work falls on the men.

It is good to be merely a clock. No frills, no arguments, no upkeep to worry about, and no responsibilities other than, of course, to keep the proper time; but then again, if no one winds me, my stopping would not be my fault, would it?

"Okay, you got me hon, we both need to get out the pen and ink and do some soul searching. We both should write to our friends that we have had for so long, and have left behind."

The fourth came too soon, according to Don and Molly. I don't know if they did not feel they were ready, or if they just felt more time would have been useful, but regardless, they insinuated that time had gone too fast.

I am quite excited about the party. I have not heard a really interesting tidbit of information since I have been here, other than that about the fighters.

A knock came on the door at precisely 3:15 PM. I had just gonged the hours a few minutes before the arrival of these first guests. It was Catherine and Julius, and that sweet little four-year old, Mable Ann. What a marvel these humans are as they seem to change from year to year. Strangely, Molly always seems the same, at least to me she does.

Catherine was fashionably dressed in an ensemble that came slightly more than five inches below her knee and it was very colorful with its red, white, and blue. I understood her to say, "It was a difficult job of sewing, but I loved the pattern."

I have no idea what that meant, but she looked quite lovely. Julius wore his white, collarless shirt, no necktie, and on his arms he had those awful elastic things above the elbow. I wondered if he ever removed them and if not, why his circulation wasn't cut off at the elbow!

Mable Ann was the image of her mother when she was at that age. The same dark brown curl that had adorned each side of her mother's face was there, falling from her forehead and stopping just above her large brown and inquisitive eyes.
An intriguing happiness radiated from them as they nested marvelously on each side of her upturned nose and over the crooked little mouth that turned up on each side forming a permanent smile.

Mable Ann looked up at her grandparent. "Good evening Grandmother and Grandfather. Thank you for inviting me."

As though they had been struck dumb, they just stood and admired the little one, so captivated by what she said that they were unable to speak. In all of the years I have been a witness to the family, there has always been abundant love not always found in families, at least the ones I have witnessed.

Don leaned down and picked her up and held her close to his body.

"You are an angel! Your grandmother and I are so glad to be close to you, and to be able to watch as you grow into a young lady."

Molly moved close to them both and touched her little granddaughter on her head, then kissed her on the cheek.

"We love you Mable Ann. We think that you are beautiful, just like your mommy."

Catherine broke the ecstasy of the moment as she moved inside the door pulling Julius along like a small wooden wagon.

"Okay, that is enough sugar coating for now, is there any room left for two plain people, like us?"

Molly hugged both Catherine and Julius as they came through the doorway into the parlor.

"My goodness Catherine, we were just so taken with Mable Ann's comment..." she hesitated for a moment, "well, overwhelmed would be the right word I believe."

"Overwhelmed indeed," Don agreed.

They made their way into the parlor where there was a subtle breeze that came across the room from the open window. The afternoon's heat was giving way to the cooler air the evening was ushering in. The family was prepared for a rewarding evening when another knock was heard An older woman was met and ushered into the parlor, a woman I had heard about, but had never seen.

"Well, I see the children have arrived ahead of me! I had hoped to be first, but I can see I am not!"

With her arm almost attached to his, Don escorted her into the room.

Molly greeted her as they entered, "Anna, it is wonderful to have you here. I assume you have been in this house before and do not need a tour of it?"

Anna looked directly at her, "Yes I have, thank you. You make a person feel very welcome Molly. I think Julius made a wise choice marrying into such a fine family."

"Mrs. Jepsen, we are humbled to have you as our guest. Our last visit was much too short, but now, being here permanently, I want you to know we love you and hope to see a lot more of you now."

Even I could see that the flowery speech was almost too much. Such honey should come from bees so easily! It appeared that humans thrive on such nonsense and it was truly important to them. But then, if they were happy, I was happy. (I was just glad that sticky conversation didn't drip onto my finish and ruin it as they spoke!)

Don, with Anna still on his arm, looked at Molly and pointed to the door.

"I think I hear footsteps coming up the walk, I'll attend to it."

Molly walked through the hall to the open front door and found Val, and his wife Mae, were about to knock.

"Do come in, it is wonderful to see you both again. Your mother has just arrived, with your brother and Catherine."

Val answered her, "I was getting prepared to knock. You have a very nice place here Molly; it is all right to call you Molly, isn't it?"

Molly hesitated before she timidly answered, "Of course, I would not have it any other way."

As Val and Mae entered the living room, Mable Ann dashed across the room and leaped into her uncle's arms. She gave a gentle kiss to his cheek, then, she stretched to do the same to Mae.

With her cherubic voice, she told them, "We are so glad you could come."

You could see the pride well up in both parents and grandparents. Mable Ann was the favorite of the family. Being the only child, she should most certainly be the most adored.

Don found favorable seating for Anna and was just about to speak when another knock sounded. I could hear him walk to the front door, and it squeaked as he opened it.

"Welcome Sam. I assume this is your fiancée Kathleen, would that be correct?"

"Yes sir Mr. Holscomb, this is Kathleen."

I could hear Don take a step backward to admire her before he spoke, "You are indeed much prettier than Sam has told us."

Kathleen coyly answered, "Thank you Mr. Holscomb, but I am sure you overstate."

As they entered the living room I could see what he had been talking about. Kathleen was a lithe young lady of average height with flaming red hair and eyes as blue as pools of water fresh from a spring. The few freckles that were sprinkled across the bridge of her nose brought attention to her delicate mouth that was small and unpretentious. It complimented her slightly turned up nose. Indeed she was priceless in her striking beauty.

Sam, on the other hand, was typical of the men I had seen so often in their youth. He was straight, but not overly tall, with a dark complexion. His dark brown eyes danced as he looked at his lovely Kathleen, and a mischievous expression seemed to be a part of his makeup. They were a handsome couple and the love between them was felt the moment they entered the room.

I was so accustomed to seeing Don stand by the fireplace with a brandy that I expected him to take that stance once more. I soon realized that the brandy was replaced by a glass of wine. As I came to understand later, the Wine Growers Association was just down the street a short distance. Many of the families in the area grew grapes, and when they harvested them, they sold them to the Council Bluffs Wine Growers Association. Their fine table wine, called Betty Anne Concord Grape Wine, was then sold to the many families in the area at a reasonable price.(10)

While the wine was poured into the glasses of those who desired it, Don proposed a toast.

"Molly and I have been blessed in many ways, during the past year, but no blessing has been more wonderful than this. Our being with all of you, here, in this wonderful town of Council Bluffs is special… may God bless and keep you all."

I was delighted to hear Don make his toast. It was good for me to be here and not left back in Waterbury for another auction. I assumed that the toast included me, even if I could not hoist a glass or drink the wine.

As the family sat about the room and talked, I discovered I wasn't listening like I used to. Instead I was watching everyone. The talk was just "getting acquainted conversation," and not too interesting. As a matter of fact it was quite boring, that is until Sam asked Julius a question.

"Who do you think will win today?"

Julius braced himself against the back of his chair as he sat up quite straight. "I assume you are speaking about the bout between Black Jack Johnson," then he snickered, "no relation to me of course," and then finished the sentence, "James J. Jeffries?"

"And who else might I be speaking of?"

Julius responded with, "I am sure no one else indeed. Who are you rooting for?"

Sam stood erect, as though offended, and stated, "James Jeffries of course. I certainly would not root for anyone else, at least in this fight."

"And why not?" Julius questioned.

"Why not indeed!. You do know that the Johnson fellow is of color... don't you?"

I had not heard that reference for some time. I recall that Miss Jessie, and her workers at the restaurant, were called folks of color from time to time. I never could figure that out. Was I, since I was Walnut, of color as well? What about Golden Oak, Dark Mahogany, White Pine, and the rest, are they all colored too? None of us in the wooden class of clocks, and furniture, have ever given a second thought to color, all we knew is that we were all wood!

"I am not sure that "being of color" has any value here Sam. Both men are fighters, both men are of the United States, both men are...well you know...equal, aren't they?"

Sam hesitated, being taken off guard by the answer.

"I see what you mean Julius, but after all, there is a difference, don't you agree?"

"No, I don't. We live here by the railroad. Tell me, where would the railroad be without those hard working black men, or those dedicated Mexican laborers? Aren't they all equal and working side by side?"

"Ah yes, working side by side. Have you not noticed the engineers are the white fellows like you and me? Have you not noticed that most of the laborers are those red-skinned folks from Mexico, or that the softer jobs, like the waiters and such in the cars, are generally those black folks?"

"Yes, I have noticed, so?"

"There is no "so" to it. The white folks have the higher paying jobs, the Mexican folks the next and the black folks the least. That proves that what I said is right!"

Julius hesitated. He didn't want to argue in front of the family, nor did he want to humiliate his friend over a foolish disagreement.

"I think we should just wait and see who wins the fight."

Sam sat down, still a bit red-faced, "You are right. We'll wait and see."

He stopped talking for a moment; he looked at the fireplace, then the floor. Apparently gaining his equilibrium, he changed the subject of the fighters to the communication or the fight.

"Did you know they are going to put this on the wire from Reno, Nevada, out to all of the radio stations, like the one we have right here in Omaha?"

"Yes I'm aware of it. We'll switch on the radio at my house later."

Don, who had been exceedingly quiet during this match of words, rose from his chair and spoke.

"You know, we have one of the boxes right here in the parlor. When the time comes, we could switch it on. I'm not too old for the fight game." *Don turned toward Val, who was sitting quietly on the settee,*

"Would you like to hear the fight as well?"

Poor Val was pulled into the middle of the discussion without warning. I knew that he worked at the post office, where I assume much gentler folks than carpenters and architects worked. Then I saw a distasteful look on his wife's face.

Val didn't think before he answered. "I'd love to hear it. We fellows at the post office have already made wagers on the outcome."

Like a bolt of lightning hit the place, Mae became outraged and stared at him with a look that could kill.

"What do you mean you 'wagered' on the outcome. You know I don't abide with gambling"… She side glanced at Don, "or drinking for that matter." "Furthermore, I don't know that we have enough time or money for that nonsense."

"Now, Mae, "Anna interrupted the fray, "men have to have some means to let out their frustration. They don't sew or knit you know!"

"Well I never! I can't believe you are taking sides with these men, mother Anna."

"I am not siding with anyone, Mae. It is just that men have to have an outlet too, and if it is someone else doing the fighting, what harm is there?"

"It just isn't proper and that's that."

Mae left the room and went out on the front porch with Molly following her, hoping to soothe her ragged nerves.

Anna continued speaking after they left.

"Since Molly is doing what she is so good at, how about the four of us turning that box on, and you too, Kathleen, if you wish,?"

Val had time to regroup his thoughts and overcome the embarrassment his wife has bestowed upon him. With everyone in agreement, the group waited for Don to turn on the apparatus. I waited impatiently to hear what would be coming out of the box and I was determined to try and understand this phenomena. The introductions came from the box, and I heard this man's excited voice.

"Ladies and Gentlemen, Welcome to the fight of the century. Today we are watching, and you are listening, to a round by round description of this "no limit" bout between none other than, that fighter known as the Galveston Giant, that six foot five inch, over two hundred pounder, Black Jack Johnson and the all time, retired favorite of the boxing world, James J. Jeffries. The time the fight started was at 1:00 PM, Western Mountain Time, here in beautiful Reno, Nevada. The final rounds are about to take place after a break between the fighters. We are approaching the 45th round and both fighters are showing the wear and tear of the bout.

Jeffries is considerably older than his opponent, the Galveston "Giant," but he has been hanging in there. Ah, there's the sound of the bell.

Both fighters are coming out of their corners. It appears that Jeffries has lost that bouncy step he had during most of the fight as he comes from his corner. Johnson is coming forward like a train engine with his fists held upward to protect his chin. Oh, there was a blow to the body by Jeffries, and another to the side, just above the kidney. Johnson moved forward and took hold of Jeffries with his left arm and punched him in the face with his right, then another and another. Jeffries is faltering, but wait, there, Johnson just took a blow to the midsection and Jeffries is loose from Johnson's grip. Another blow to the midsection and Jeffries has been forced against the ropes. Johnson moved to his right and avoided a blow to the chest while at the same time slammed Jeffries with a hard left to the jaw. Jeffries is stumbling and Johnson is moving in for the kill. A right, then a left, and another right as Jeffries stumbles against the ropes. The referee is holding Johnson back letting Jeffries regain his balance, there now again before he has a chance to regain his composure Johnson has struck again, this time it looks like a tough one for Jeffries. He has fallen. He's down folks and it doesn't look good at all for him. Johnson is standing over him and the referee is trying to move him away. Johnson has both hands raised high in the air in a signal of his win. The crowd is in an uproar. Oh my goodness, the police are having a problem with a few fellows in the front row. It appears they are throwing things into the ring as the referee is working on the count. He just counted to ten. Ladies and Gentlemen, it's all over, the Galveston Giant has won the bout, Jeffries is still down."

It sounded very frightening. I think that the giant (apparently a big fellow) won but I wondered if it was fair. If he was a giant, was the other fellow just an ordinary man? It never made sense to me why two humans would want to hit each other anyhow. I used to be concerned when the men at the clock- shop picked up a hammer or a saw, but I never saw them hitting each other.

Julius seemed triumphant when he said, "Well it's over, the giant won."

Val spoke, quietly. "I will never hear the end of this. When Mae finds out I lost a whole fifty-cents on this, she is not going to talk to me for at least a week!"

Don could not help but sarcastically remark, "And that would be bad?"

I heard subtle laughter at the remark, but for one reason or another it didn't appear Val was laughing with the rest of the men. Anna apparently thought it quite humorous as her laughter filled the room, along with the men. Kathleen just smiled quietly.

In an attempt to overcome the comment of his father-in-law, Julius spoke up. "I just hope that everyone takes this like they should, just a fight between to consenting adults for money and the crown of the game."

"Surely they will, won't they? Kathleen asked with her quiet little voice.

Mae's abrupt appearance, with her unsolicited question, caught everyone's attention.

"Well, what have we here?"

No doubt worried that she might have overheard the previous conversation, Val spoke up.

"Nothing my love, nothing at all. We were just about to check on you, out on the porch, to see what you and Molly were up to."

"I see. I could have sworn I heard laughter a short time back. Would that be accurate?"

"Yes dear, yes it would be, Don told us a very funny story."

Everyone in the room laughed inwardly at the pretense Val was putting on to humor Mae. One thing was for sure, Mother Jepsen was more like one of the boys than I had assumed she would be.

"Well Molly, did you and Mae sort out the problems of the world while you were gone?"

Mae answered, rather than Molly.

"Let's put it this way, we, being ladies," *she hesitated and looked straight at Anna,* "well let me put this another way, we decided that fighting was a disgusting sport for ladies, but unfortunately not for some women."

Someone made a strange noise that sounded like "Harrumph." Then Julius spoke up, "Let's all have a cup of tea."

Everyone was in agreement so Catherine and Molly went into the kitchen where they removed the large kettle of hot tea from the stove, poured it into two beautiful teapots, and took them both into the living room. All too soon, the tea was served and drank, the group left for their own homes, and all that remained was the silence that gave tranquility to the sleepy couple. Their first party had come to an end, and the mess had been cleaned up.

They decided on a small snack, instead of a dinner, as so many finger sandwiches had been consumed during the afternoon.

They discovered during the course of the evening, according to the many conversations, that dinner was at noon, there was no lunch, (unless you carried it in a lunch pail) and supper was now the evening meal. I felt it was a strange thing to find that Iowa had traditions of its own that changed all that I had become accustomed to in Connecticut. The next morning came sooner than expected, and as Molly was preparing breakfast, she turned on the talking box in the parlor.

The scratchy sound made listening difficult, but I could make out that there was a terrible riot taking place in Omaha. She fine-tuned the apparatus to get a better sound, and I soon discovered there were riots in several other places as well, and all because a black man had won the fight. How childish for humans to act. I thank goodness it didn't affect Council Bluffs and our lives. (11)

There was some young man living in Omaha, a fellow named Henry Fonda. His name only came up as he had, what would be considered, a perfect window from which to watch these foolish people as they fought, and a reporter asked if he could watch from there as well. He saw them lynch a black man whom they accused of rape, although as it was determined later, there apparently was no proof. It was done for really no reason what so ever, except for the fact the man was "of color!"

CHAPTER 18

In general, the news of the day was quite
bleak, that is until Molly received a wonderful letter
from her sister-in-law back in Connecticut. A
surprise changed Molly's attitude from loneliness for
her friends, to joy as she read that one of her two
nephews was getting married, and the other was
completing his second year of college. Claudia wrote
further that she wished that she had not gone to be
with her relatives, but instead, had moved to Iowa, to
be with the Molly and Don
Molly was determined to answer the letter
that had brought back memories of the good times
they had before Don's brother passed, but time passed
and the letter seemed to be forgotten.
1909 came and went, and with nothing
earthshaking happening around us. There was not a
log of guests, and I was thankful for the talking box.
A fellow named Perry made his way to
something called the North Pole. I just could not
figure out what they were talking about. I remember a
pole Molly used to speak of that she used.

It held up a rope that she hung clothes on, but for the life of me, I don't recall there being one for the North and another for some other direction.

The projections made in 1908 of a new era coming, (whatever an era is supposed to be) were apparently overrated; perhaps this "era" thing is just slower than these humans thought in its coming.

The Wright Brothers sold an airplane to some branch of the government called the Signal Corps. As I understood, from my eavesdropping, they were going to use it in preparation for their fighting. Something called war. I will never understand these humans. Why do they like fighting so? If there is no war, why prepare for one?

The month brightened somewhat when Don decided to look at cars. There was, according to the conversations that I overheard, not a great selection of them in Council Bluffs.

"Molly," Don looked across the breakfast table, "I think the time has come for me to look at cars."

Molly glanced up from her reading, "Why? We don't have anywhere to go that we can't walk to."

"We might go further if we had a car. Julius' brother lives north of here in a place called Missouri Valley. Little Mable has never ridden in one, and once in a while, it might be nice to get out of town and see what's happening around us, and take her with us. Don't you agree?"

Molly just shook her head in amazement at his comment. "You know as well as I do it wouldn't make any real difference what I think. If you have made up your mind..."

Don interrupted, "Hon, now you know I wouldn't just go out and do something like buying a car, without you agreeing."

"Oh, really," Molly answered rather harshly, "the last time you decided on something like that, you came home with it. Then you told me that we had to be get rid of our horse, old Bessie. Do you remember that?"

Don stammered, "Well, yes, but I needed it for work, don't' you remember?"

Without answering, Molly continued her commentary on the car business, "And all you did was shout bad words when it wouldn't start. Do you remember when the crank came backward and almost broke your arm?"

Don continued his positive thoughts, "But they are built better now."

"So you say! Why don't you take Julius, and go look at what's available. You may change your mind after looking at them, and their problems."

Don realized that he had been chided, so he walked next door to discuss the idea with his son-in-law. I could see that the two of them were on the same wavelength when it came to automobiles. I could also see them through the window as it was a short distance to Julius's front porch. Their smiles radiated in the sun as they discussed the new automobiles that were available. The next day Molly admitted to Catherine that she never saw the two of them look happier than when they went shopping for a car.

Don had mentioned several times he would like to see that new car called the Hudson. He wasn't sure there was a dealer there, but insisted they should go downtown and investigate the matter. It wasn't long before the two returned with a disdainful look. The happiness turned to sadness as they returned home.

"I'm home Molly." Don entered the front door.

That small sentence that I used to hear nightly when he came home from work, now lacked the luster and happy sound it had in Waterbury.

"Well, how did it go? Are we going to own a new motorcar or not?" Molly was teasing, and jousting with words at the same time.

"Not right away I guess. There is not a dealer in town. There is talk about one coming into Omaha sometime within the next year or so but to get one of those new Hudsons now I would have to have it shipped! That would not only be expensive, but who would repair it if it needed work done on it?"

Molly smiled to herself as she answered him, "Well, you have to be sensible honey. You know they do break down from time to time, and the newer ones may take special tools or something. The old pliers and screwdriver, along with a piece of wire, may not work anymore."

Molly was teasing, but at the same time she was being practical.

Don was a bit mopey; I could tell from his words that he was not going to give up just because there wasn't a dealer for that particular make. After all, as he had argued in the past, there are other cars around. There was the Maxwell, the Ford, the Chevrolet, the Cadillac, and who knows what other brands were out there that he was not aware of?

For the next month or so, he and Julius poured over the advertisements, talked to men who had purchased new motorcars and asked where they got them, and where they had them serviced. It became an obsession with the two of them. They would sit for hours just talking about those motorcar things, but for the life of me I don't know why. After all, motorcars were just another bothersome thing without real value. It seemed to me that they were just something you could bury in the building out back, pour money into, and then waste time trying to find somewhere to go! Automobiles are totally unlike me because I am useful. Without me, folks would not know when to get up, or when to go to bed; they would not know if guests were on time or late. Without my chimes the silence would be deafening, except for that absurd train whistle that sounds like it is right outside the living room window.

"You know, father Holscomb, I think we are going to have to find another kind of automobile. Waiting for that Hudson motorcar might be a long wait. What would you think about you and me buying one of those new trucks, instead? I could use it in my carpentry business, and you could use it for whatever you wanted as well."

Don looked away from the brochure he had been admiring as though in deep thought. I have seen that look before and it meant he was about to say something of interest.

"I thought about that before, but there is a catch."

"A catch, what do you mean?"

Don looked into Julius's blue eyes as he spoke, "You have a little daughter who happens to be my little granddaughter. Now let's assume you, or better yet, we, would like to go somewhere and take her along. Where would she ride?"

Julius set his finger under his chin, "I guess you do have a point. There is only room for two people on that one seat, unlike the two-seat car we have been looking for. Oh well, it was just a thought."

"Yes, but a good thought." Don added. "You do need transport for lumber from and to the mill, or roof materials and such. Have you considered a horse drawn wagon for that kind of work?"

Julius smiled. "Yes I have, but I have to weigh the time involved. You know that today time is money. I work by the job, so the more quickly I can get the job finished, the better off I am."

Don responded, "That is true, but the horse is a reliable creature and probably could haul more in a large wagon than the truck could."

"Yes," Julius countered, "but I would have to have a place for food and shelter, it would require extra time to take care of, with currying and such, and of course, there is the matter of having to also buy a wagon that would fit the need."

"Yes, that is true." Don seemed to stare off into no man's land, "I suppose, in the long run, the upkeep may be more. You do have to remember though, that those tires would probably only last a few months with that kind of load."

"True, very true, but then maybe I could use metal wheels instead of those new rubber ones, and just drive responsibly. Remember the speed limit is 15 miles per hour on the road and even less in town."

I was astounded to hear about the speed of things. To even consider moving at that rate made me nauseous, and I am just a clock! Imagining 15 miles in just one hour was overwhelming. Can you imagine what would happen if a wheel would break, or if the car would go careening off somewhere at that speed? After what happened to Don's brother, well...I would be worried if I were able to do so.

The days continued and the discussions became more frequent. The ladies were getting a bit tired of the whole thing.

"Do you think the two of them will ever get over this motorcar silliness mother?"

Molly sat her cup of tea on the table, finished swallowing the remainder of a cookie after chewing it thoroughly.

"Probably not until they decide to go and buy one of those things."

"That is what I am thinking too. Next thing you know, they will each want one! Then we'll have to put up with two of them shouting when the cranks don't start the engines, or a tire goes flat, or who knows what else? Besides, motorcars belch out smoke that gets our clothing dirty and sooty, as a train engine might, and at the same time creating a mess with the spare parts and tools laying all over the place."

Molly laughed, "It probably won't be that bad Catherine, but you are right about part of it. I remember hearing some rather foul language emitting from the barn when our tin- lizzie wouldn't start, even after being cranked. One time that crank decided to have a mind of its own and went backward just as the car backfired and almost broke your father's arm."

Catherine stared in disbelief at her mother. "Oh my goodness, could that happen to Julius?"

Molly halted her laughter after seeing that she had started a worry line on her daughter's face.

"Don't worry, Catherine, I am sure that by now, the folks that make those automobiles will have corrected that feature."

"I certainly hope so. If Julius were to get hurt...well, I just hope you are right."

There were many conversations similar to that one that continued to take place as we waited to see what Don and Julius were going to do. Time did not stand still for Julius though, as there was work to be done every day in the carpenter trade. He was extremely busy.

Don busied himself with the yard and the gardening, but he continued to pour over the various advertisements for automobiles. Then one day, he stood up, and while holding the newspaper at full length of his arms, he called out to his sweetheart.

"Molly!" he shouted. "Honey, I think I have found it at last."

"Found what?" Molly asked enthusiastically.

"The car honey, the car I have been waiting for."

"For goodness sake, I thought it was something important!" Molly turned and walked back down the hall to the kitchen.

Following quickly behind, Don was holding the paper in front of him, and shaking it, like he might an unruly child.

"But Molly," he persisted, "Don't you see? I have found the perfect car for us, and we can afford it too!"

Molly, with sarcasm in her voice, responded to his comment. "Really, are they giving them away?"

"Now Molly, there is no need to be nasty. Of course they are not giving them away, and I have been frugal this year; besides we made the extra money on the sale of the house in Connecticut and saved it for this purpose, didn't we?"

"Well, yes I suppose we did..."

"Just listen to this." Don proceeded to read from the advertisement. "The Maxwell, the car of tomorrow. Can you imagine driving the motor car that went from coast to coast while driven by a gentile woman? Can you imagine feeling secure in a motor car that has two leather stuffed seats for comfort, and with the safety of a pressed steel framework?
Your new touring car can cost less than $700.00, including shipping from Chicago by freight car! The Maxwell is the motor car of the future. Contact your nearest agent now!"

The look on Molly's face must have been worth seeing. I could not see her from my fireplace 'station in life,' but I could imagine that by the sound of her voice when she answered him what that expression must be.

"It sounds to me like you are sold on the Maxwell. That would be the United States Motor Car Company, would it not?"

"Why, yes it is Molly. I had no idea that you..."

"Of course you didn't. Catherine and I have to pick up after you two all the time, and we can both read you know! I saw that ad last night after the paper boy delivered it."

Don was amazed at her knowledge. "You mean that you already knew about…"

Molly's tone was sharp, "Of course I already knew, and I spoke to Catherine about it earlier this morning when we had tea on the porch. All she could say was, "Thank goodness, maybe now they will settle down!"

Later that day I could hear Don, on the new phone in the hallway, speaking to someone in a rather loud tone.

"Hello, …what? I said hello, …can you hear me? Yes, I'm calling from Council Bluffs in Iowa. Yes, that's right, Council Bluffs. You say there is a dealer where?... He does?... Right here? That is wonderful, thank you so much. Good bye."

It was a good thing the lines were at long last installed and now long distance phone service was available. (As I recall, Don hated this new convenience not so long ago)

He hung up the phone and rushed back to the kitchen. Molly could see that he was as excited as a child with a new toy.

"Hon, there is a dealer, right here in town, that can order them from the factory and have a new one here within the month. Isn't that wonderful?"

Molly raised her head and looked at Don questionably, "If they have to order it, and have it shipped, how can you be sure they can service it?"

"Because, the factory man in Detroit told me so."

"Detroit! Do you mean you called all the way up there without us talking about it?"

I could almost see the perspiration on his forehead when he answered her.

"Well, yes, I suppose I did. But you see Molly…"

"Yes I see. You can call up there, but you think it is terrible if I want to call my friends in Waterbury, right?"

"Gosh hon, you are right. I'm sorry. I just got so excited about finding that car I have been waiting on, I forgot about long distance charges."

Molly, knowing she had pricked his conscience, barely smiled as she told him, "I'm not mad at you sweetheart, but of course I will have to call Margaret and tell her of your new purchase, won't I?"

I could hear her walk across the floor. The kiss on his cheek resounded almost through the whole house.

Don came into the living room and went immediately to the small corner cabinet where he kept two glasses, and a small flask of Betty Anne wine. Before he had even had the opportunity to pour it, Molly entered the room.

"You forgot to tell me. What is this dealer's name?"

Don turned to face her, "I guess I didn't, did I? It is the Council Bluffs Automobile Company. They are on Broadway, downtown."

"I see, "Molly answered, "and are they a regular Maxwell dealer?"

"I didn't ask."

"And why didn't you ask? You would have asked before you bought anything, when you were with The Brass Company."

"Why am I getting the third degree, have I done something you don't approve of?"

Fortunately, before the debate reached a fever point, the door to the front porch opened and Julius appeared.

"Hope I'm not interrupting something important. I was just wondering, did you find anything new on our search?"

Molly stood to leave the room.

"You boys go ahead. I have dinner to prepare."

Don, somewhat bewildered, remarked, "Glad you came in Julius. Do I seem the same to you as I did before? I mean am I any different than when you first met me?"

Julius seemed reluctant to answer. "I don't think so. At least I haven't noticed, why do you ask?"

Don answered quietly, as though it was an afterthought, "Oh it's not important, just something Molly said a minute ago."

He regrouped his thoughts, then continued with more exuberance.

" Now, for the important stuff. I think I found what we are looking for!"

Julius's curiosity was aroused. "Really, what did you find?"

"I found this," and he handed the newspaper advertisement to Julius.

"Wow! A Maxwell, pretty fancy car don't you think?"

He didn't let on that Catherine had already told him about the advertisement.

"Yes it is, and the price is tremendous, only around $700.00, and delivered too!"

Julius laid the paper down, "Can I have a small glass of whatever you are having?"

Don answered quickly, "Oh for goodness sake, where are my manners?"

Julius picked the paper up again and perused the advertisement more closely. Don stood, and then he walked to the corner cabinet, and removed the Betty Anne Wine and poured the sparkling liquid into the other glass that was there.

"It says here, that four women drove the 1908 model all the way across the country in just

48 days. That is really astounding isn't it? Can you imagine going at that speed?

Julius took a pencil and a small tablet out of his jacket pocket and did some figuring. He double checked his figures, then took a breath, and then a short drink before he laid the pencil down. He looked at his father-in-law's face.

"Do you realize that those women averaged seventy-nine miles every day? That's unheard of. Gosh, seventy-nine miles! They had to be flying didn't they?"

Both men sat back in their chairs and looked up at the ceiling. The thought of going so fast lingered in the air as they sat silently, with their untouched drink in their hands. Their dreams of travel had overtaken all responsibility and common sense.

Molly entered the room as they were gazing into space. They sat with that fixed look, of a private dream world, on their faces.

"I hate to have to bring you two back to reality, but my dinner is done and I bet Catherine is expecting you too, don't you think so Julius?"

Dreamily, Julius answered as he slowly arose from his chair, "Yes mam, of course you are right... just think seventy-nine miles in one day. Gosh."

As he sauntered off toward the door, Don returned to reality. He stood, put his glass on the corner cabinet pull-out, and followed Molly into the

kitchen without a word being spoken. Dinner
was eaten in total silence.

   The following morning, Molly was up at 6:30.
She had helped Catherine gather some eggs and clean
them, check the icebox, and feed the cat. Breakfast was
about to be put on the table when a sleepy Don
entered the room.

   "Good morning honey. Did you have a
good night's sleep? It seemed to me you tossed
and turned a lot and you kept saying, "Gosh
Alice, that was sure great." What were you
dreaming, and who is Alice?"

   Still half-asleep, Don didn't attempt an
answer, "I'm not awake yet. Can I have some
coffee first."

   Acting a bit miffed, Molly pushed for
more information, "No, you can't, not until you
tell me who Alice is."

   Don had to think for a few minutes, then
he replied, "I guess that would be the Alice
person who drove the car across America. I
don't know any Alice personally."

   He must have said the right thing, because I
could hear the tea being poured into his cup and the
shuffling of silverware on the table.

   "That is a good answer. I remember
reading about that lady in the ad, Alice Ramsey,
or something like that, and it's a good thing for
you."

   Molly turned toward the kitchen stove so

Don could not see her smiling. "I suppose all of that twisting and turning was due to that silly motor car too, wasn't it?"

Bewildered, but more awake, Don answered, "Yes, I suppose so."

As that last answer slid from Don's lips, Julius stuck his head inside the kitchen door. He wasn't too sure whether he was welcome or not until Molly saw him and insisted he come in, sit down, and have breakfast with them.

"Thanks mother Holscomb, but I have already had breakfast with Catherine and Mable Ann. I couldn't eat another bite, but I might have a cup of coffee with you."

"That would be fine," then Molly added, "and just so you don't worry, I'm not disgusted with either of you, just keeping your father-in-law in line, which is a full time job."

She continued smiling to herself as she poured the coffee, then she gave Don a light, but meaningful, kiss on his cheek.

CHAPTER 19

*The furor caused by the fight on the fourth of
the month was still raging in Omaha, especially on
the south side of Farnam Street.*

Council Bluffs seemed quiet and unscathed. It seemed to me that these quarrels could be better settled with words than with fists. These humans could take a lesson from us, the wooden society. The only noise we make is when our door or drawers are slammed, or when someone blows into what is known as a woodwind instrument.
(Incidentally I have never seen nor heard one, but I know about them from minor conversations that took place at the restaurant so long ago.)

"I do think that we should go to Omaha and see the Hudson before we do anything else."

It was as though Julius had read Don's mind.

"Why do you say that?" He was curious why Julius came up with the idea.

"Well, there's a new dealership getting ready to open there called Guy Smith Automotive. They are completing the building now, and Guy might have a deal or two up his sleeve."

"In that case I guess we better get hopping then since we will have to take the streetcar across the Douglas Street Bridge into Omaha."

It was easy to see that Don was eager to go. The car shopping had begun with the Maxwell, and even I could feel the tension of the situation.

They grabbed their caps, to protect their heads from the hot summer sun, and then they left through the front door. I could see them as they walked briskly away. I wished that I could have gone with them since I remember that the Sixth Street streetcar connection was across the street from the railway station, where Don had first entered Council Bluffs. It was also the place I was taken off the train, and I remember that quite well. The conductor had stopped the train, and as the passengers were disembarking, he opened the baggage car and handed down some luggage for the passengers. With some difficulty, he and his helper lifted the large trunk and moved it to the car door's edge hoping someone would take it the rest of the way down. I recall Don looking anxiously toward the open doors to the car.

"Isn't there another smaller wooden, slatted crate there for me?"

The conductor looked at the colored fellow, who stood on the inside of the car helping him, with a discouraging look. The poor fellow almost wilted as he started to dig furiously into the remaining luggage piled in front of him. Then a smile came on his face as he found my crate, and he pulled it from close to the door, but from behind some smaller packages that were there.

"Here it is boss, I got it." He told the conductor. *The black man seemed both pleased, and relieved, that he had found it. The conductor was relieved too, but neither of them as much as I was to get out of the sweltering heat of the car. I watched the whole episode and could I have spoken I could have alleviated the whole situation much sooner. Don knew the wrath of Molly would certainly come to the forefront should I not have been located.*

"This reminds me of the first time I met your friend Sam."

"Really, why is that father Holscomb?"

"You know, I think we are going to disband with the 'father Holscomb' title. It makes me feel like I should be a priest or something. How about just 'Don' instead?"

Julius was relieved.

"I am so glad you said that Don. I was beginning to dislike the sound of it myself. You have made life much easier and now I really feel like one of the family, as well as your friend."

"It's settled then." Don changed the subject, "I assume you know all about the switching of the streetcars and what we are going to be looking for in Omaha, right?"

"I have been to Omaha many times. It may seem a little backward to you at first, but it is a growing city, a bit larger than Council Bluffs. You know the stockyards have helped this city a lot. It is such a shame that the city fathers of Council Bluffs didn't have the foresight to allow the cattle industry here instead of there. Of course our Aldermen just could not stand the smell of a slaughter house and stock yards."

"You sound like a politician in the making." Don smiled at Julius and patted him on his back.

"Someday soon perhaps, but not today, today is car shopping day!" Julius was smiling ear to ear. He was pleased to be with his father-in-law, and now felt more like an equal.

I had just chimed four in the afternoon when the two of them returned. I had been watching while Molly and Catherine worked in the yard, and as little Mable Ann played in a sandbox Julius had made for her. As the men approached the side yard between the two houses, Molly stood up, after being perched on her knees, to greet them both. The breeze made her skirt move from side to side keeping time with the day lilies as they swayed in unison.

The window was open allowing that same summer breeze to bring their voices into the living room. I could not only see them through the lace-curtained windows, but I could also hear them clearly. Molly was puzzled that no car was in the street in front of the houses.

"Well, I don't see a car. What did you find out?"

"To make a long story short, we just couldn't find what we wanted." Don answered.

"Mother and I thought you two had figured it all out in advance, and would come home broke, but happy."

Molly, relieved, but not wanting to show it, asked, "Well, since the car is not here, pray tell us what happened."

Catherine interrupted, "First, why don't we just sit on the back porch and have a lemonade, then maybe your throats will open up enough, after such a parching day, to tell us what has happened."

Julius responded quickly, "Yes, that would be an excellent idea. Don and I are both tired and dry."

I noticed that Julius had called his father-in-law by his first given rather than the accepted 'Father Holscomb'.

Catherine looked at her husband questioningly. "Since when do we call dad, Don?"

Don answered the question, lifting the weight from his son-in-law.

"I told your husband that I was feeling quite embarrassed with the 'father Holscomb' business and would like it much better if he were to just call me Don."

*Before anyone else could speak, Molly
addressed Julius.*

"Then I assume it would be all right for
you to call me Molly, as I am not a nun so
'mother' may sound good to some, but
somewhat condescending to me."

*Everyone laughed and the agreement was
made, that from now on, the names would be Don
and Molly, or Dad and Mom, no more mother this,
and father that.*

*Catherine had made some lemonade earlier in
anticipation of a hot afternoon. She poured the
concoction into four glasses from the kitchen cabinet
in the kitchen and Don and Julius carried them to the
porch. The foursome sat in the cane porch chairs and
sipped their drinks. They all seemed to agree, with an
"ah-h-h," how good it was to have such refreshments
on this hot day.*

"Let me start from the beginning. First, I
have to say Julius really knows his way around.
We had to switch cars at Broadway and Main
streets. The second car was a larger one that
went on into Omaha. That Missouri River is a
threatening looking bit of water. It is not only
wide, but brown with mud and moving like it
was being regurgitated from some beast below
the surface.

I can't image the first settlers forging that
thing, and just being pulled by ropes and
oxen."

He took a drink of his lemonade, then continued his description of the trip.

"Anyhow, getting on with it, we took the streetcar to almost the western-most end of town, at Twenty-Fourth Street and Farnam Streets, where a gentleman, by the name of Guy Smith, was building a structure to sell the new Hudson Motor Cars from."

Julius chimed in, "Yes, it was a very nice building, and extremely large as well."

Don continued, "Mr. Smith was there, but tied up with the overseeing of the workmen. He didn't have a lot to say, except to let us know he was disappointed that he had nothing to show us, or even to actually tell us about."

Molly interrupted, "I would think he would have had something to say about those Hudson Motor Cars he is going to sell?"

"Hon, this is not Connecticut you know. We have to get accustomed to being here on the plains."

"The plains?" Julius sounded offended.

"I didn't mean it that way. I'm sorry Julius. I just meant that some folks aren't as astute on business yet, as they have..."

"Don. I am not offended, just hadn't heard the area here described that way before."

Molly commented, "Let's get back to the motor car subject."

"Yes, let's." Catherine agreed.

Everyone remained very quiet for what seemed to me a terribly long period of time. Each with a glass in hand and sipping their lemonade quietly and carefully; finally, Don broke the silence.

"The only thing Guy told us was he had spent over $40,000.00 on the building, which is three floors in height; a ton of money on the franchise, and of course he still had people to hire and train. He hoped to have the first cars off the line to sell by Valentine's Day and would call us if we would like him to, at that time.

Catherine asked, "What did you tell him?"

"We didn't know what to say so we gave him our phone number and told him we were on the third ring on the party line. I also suggested we may be inclined to buy something earlier than that, but we would keep him in mind.'

Julius continued the story, "We also told him that we probably would not be buying this year, but who knew what tomorrow might bring."

Molly asked, "And was he happy with that?"

"No, he wasn't, but what was he to say?"

Molly sat her glass on the porch railing. "So what is the decision now?"

"Well, we stopped downtown on the way back. There is another dealer called the Council Bluffs Automobile Company, and they deal in several makes, including that new Maxwell."

"Aha, so you did find a Maxwell dealer."

Don was flustered, "Kind of."

"What do you mean, kind of'?"

"Well, he can order the car, as I think we discussed earlier, but it will take about three weeks or so."

"How much?" Molly asked.

"Somehow, I knew you would ask."

"So-o-o … how much?" Molly persisted.

Don dropped his head as he almost whispered, "Eight Hundred and forty three dollars and twenty cents… to be exact."

Molly took another swallow of her lemonade. That is a lot of money. I thought you said around Seven Hundred Dollars delivered, before."

Don turned his head rather than face her, then he almost whispered the answer.

"Well, I did; but I forgot a few things like the cost to get it here, which was more than I suspected. Then, there is that new tax on motor cars, the Government you know; then something called a preparation charge and…"

Molly tired of the long soliloquy, "So, when is it coming?"

Both Molly and Catherine knew their husbands quite well, and apparently reading their faces was an art both had perfected over their married years.

Mable Ann was standing on the doorway step listening. She smiled through a bit of dirt on her mouth. With her tiny hands covered with sand, and dirty little hands, she listened and absorbed the way that her mother and grandmother handled things. Things only women seem to understand.

"Can I have something to drink mommy?"

After she wiped the dirt away from her tiny mouth, Catherine gave her a drink out of her glass, "Thank you mommy."

She turned and made her way down the steps one at a time, then she returned to her sandbox, totally unaware that her father and her grandfather would soon have a new toy, a different one than she had seen in their yard before.

The next three weeks went by quite slowly, and both Julius and Don were like children around a candy store waiting for it to open. Then the big day arrived, August 18. It was a beautiful Thursday, with the sun shining brightly through the shades that had been drawn the night before. The temperature was quite warm for this time of year, and a hot breeze ebbed its way into the bedroom as Don raised himself up, threw his arms into the air, and produced a very wide-mouthed and loud yawn.

I could hear from my stationary perch in the parlor, as he teased Molly awake.

"Guess what today is?"

Molly slowly answered, "I don't know dear, what is it.?

"It is go get the motor car day, darlin'."

"Is that a new holiday?" Molly teased.

Don laughed, "It should be. It isn't every day one gets a new motor car is it?"

I heard him as he jumped out of bed. The sound that radiated through the floorboards was like thunder. I wondered if they were going to break. Then he came down the stairs two at a time, and all the time whistling I don't remember him doing that before so I was not accustomed to that shrill sound. It was not a gentle pleasing tone, like the chime in my works.

There was a knock on the back door and Don answered it.

"Are you ready?" A voice asked.

Don answered. "I haven't had breakfast yet, have you?"

Julius came through the screen door, letting it bounce against the little ball that was attached to the casing. "Oh, sorry about that, I didn't mean to let the door slam that way; and no, I haven't had breakfast, too excited to eat!"

"Don't worry about it, the door that is, today is a very special day."

"Yes indeed, yes indeed. I can't wait to go with you and get that new motor car."

Don turned away from the stove, "You mean you took the time off to go with me?"

Julius answered, "That's right. I didn't want to be responsible for you getting lost downtown."

"I see," Don retorted to the sarcastic remark. "You think that I am getting old, do you?"

"Oops!"

"I would think "oops" all right. You better watch out young man or I might have to whup-up on you."

The air moved as Dons hand moved in a fake attempt to strike his son-in-law for the remark. The two of them had become like father and son, and that was a good thing for everyone, even me.

Molly came down the stairs, fully dressed and ready to prepare breakfast.

"Molly, to be honest, I am too excited to eat. Would it be okay if I just skipped breakfast and ate lunch when we get back?"

"Scoot." Molly waved her apron at them. "Just go and get that motor car. I'm dying to see it."

The two of them scurried out of the kitchen and down the hall; then they dashed out of the front door like two excited children on holiday from school. Molly watched them as they walked quickly to the corner of Eighth Street and Sixteenth Avenue, then turned left by Mortensen's grocery store and disappeared.

Catherine and Mable Ann came to Molly's place shortly after Julius and had left. I couldn't remember anything being so exciting, not even when I was delivered and Molly helped unpack me from my crate.

At the same time, Catherine came through the kitchen door and asked, "Wasn't that Dad and Julius hurrying up the street?"

"Yes dear, I am afraid it was."

"Julius didn't even eat his breakfast this morning he was in such a hurry. I don't recall ever seeing him in such a hurry. That motor car must really be something."

I could hear Molly fiddling with the few dishes on the table, then moving her apron frontwards and backwards. I imagined her with her hands on each side of her hips.

"I haven't seen Don this happy in a long time. We made a plan, early on, for him to make the purchase, so the money was there for him. I am just surprised he is buying a Maxwell, since he seemed to have his heart set on that Hudson car."

Catherine looked at her mother with both admiration and concern.

"I guess he has earned it mother. I am just worried that he doesn't look as well as he has in the past."

It seemed like a very short time had passed, when the toot-toot of a horn was heard in the front of the house. Both Molly and Catherine, along with little Mable Ann, rushed to the front of the house to see their beloved men-folk driving up in a spanking new Maxwell Motor Car. The pride showed in their expression. Don turned off the switch and leaped from the motorcar and rushed to Molly's side.

Don's enthusiasm was contagious as he spoke.

"Isn't she a beauty? Boy does she handle sweetly too. It even has a wheel to steer it with. She's a pure joy to drive, compared to old Lizzy. This is a date to mark on the calendar, August 11, 1910."

Julius was just as quick to extricate himself from the passenger side. "Wait until you ride in this Catherine," he looked down at Mable Ann and continued, "and you too honey. Boy is it ever swell!"

They spoke so loudly in their excitement, that not only could I hear every word clearly, but the neighbors did as well.

Mr. Mortensen from the grocery store stepped out of the front door onto 8th street, with his stained white butcher's apron on, to see what the commotion was. "What in tarnation? Is that a new Maxwell motor car?"

"It sure is," exclaimed Don.

"Just get it, did you?"

"That's right, and you are the first to see it. What do you think?"

"Well, using that for deliveries may be faster than my old jalopy," Mr. Mortensen hesitated, and then he continued sarcastically, "of course mine is paid for." He spit on the dirt street getting rid of the snuff in his mouth.

Indignantly, Don answered, "Mine is too, I can't stand debt!" Then he added, "I guess the grocery business is doing well?"

"Yup, 'tis indeed. Young Howard will take it over one day, along with his sisters, Evelyn and Ilene. It is a fine business to leave them."

"You have a lot to be proud of. That is a beautiful house you have built next to it, too."

Don was pouring on the compliments, why I will never understand. It was clear, even to me, that the grocery man was being as belligerent as he could be. Mr. Mortensen continued, but with less contempt in his voice.

"Your son-in-law had a lot to do with that. He's was a real catch for your daughter. I suppose we are going to lose him, one of these days, to politics. I don't like that much, but I understand he's bent on doing it."

Don responded, "All we can do for these young folks, is hope and pray they do what is right, and I am sure they will."

I am so thankful for my vantage point, here in the living room, because I can see and hear just about everything that happens, in close proximity of course. Watching Don and the grocery store's owner converse and hearing what they have to say, is a marvelous thing. Sometimes I feel like I may be eavesdropping, but who would I ever be able to tell anyhow? All I get a chance to talk to are my wooden friends in our wooden language.

The men came into the house, followed by their wives, and headed straight to the kitchen.

"Well mam, Julius, and I are inclined to have that big breakfast now. What say you?"

"Is that a request or an order?"

"Now mam, I don't give no orders."

He did his best to imitate the men he heard around the Omaha stockyards, but his attempt was not that well done.

Molly and Catherine both smiled as Molly answered, "I know dear, but I have to have a little fun with you... cowboy. The she turned to her daughter, "You know Catherine, I think since the boys had so much fun buying that expensive car, perhaps we could take a look at the Sears catalogue and see what we might like to purchase for ourselves, and perhaps something special for Mable Ann as well. What do you think?"

Don spoke up. "Now hold on there you two fillies."

"What do you mean hold on? We fillies ought to be entitled to a new dress considering how we have to put up with you two."

Don smiled at Julius as he spoke.

"Well, when you put it that way, I suppose a couple of dresses for you wouldn't hurt anything."

CHAPTER 20

Molly read out loud from the new Sear's catalogue their policy on payment.

"We have discontinued making C.O.D. shipments; discontinued shipping by freight with draft on bill of lading for collection; discontinued shipping on open account or on any terms other than cash, in full, with orders, solely in the interest of our customers, with a view to naming still lower prices, giving greater values than ever before."

Molly continued with her own thoughts.

"It appears that they no longer honor any customer accounts or other means of payment. They claim they can save a lot of money doing it this way and pass that savings on to us, but I seriously doubt it. You know it is a shame there is no other place to buy, but, on the other hand, they do offer more products than anyone else. Of course when they say cash, they don't mean just bills and coins, although they would accept them; they mean money orders from the Post Office; bank drafts; and even stamps."

The ladies busied themselves by turning one page at a time and staring at the marvelous goods that were being offered.

Molly continued reading from the first page. "The freight costs are high. Coming to Iowa they are charging the minimum cost of $0.25 and as high as $0.80 if up to 100 pounds."

It seemed to me they searched for hours before they decoded what they wanted.

"Okay mother, I would like to buy this one for Mable Ann, if you don't think it is too expensive."

"Which one is that dear?" Molly looked down at the page Catherine was holding.

"No. 3842103. It is so beautiful and made with lawn too! Here, see the description."

Molly again read out loud. "Very Pretty Child's dress, made of figured lawn, short sleeves, low round neck, and collar all around edged with Valenciennec lace, lace trimmings on collar, wide hem at bottom. A very neat and dressy garment. Colors pink, or blue predominating. Price $0.75."

"It is settled then, a pink dress for our little lady. Now let's find one for ourselves."

I listened as they continued. After relentless searching they decided on what they referred to as Lady's Stylish Lawn Wash Waists, which for the life of me I could not understand how a waist could be something to wear, especially after being washed on the lawn. They said they would be practical to take care of. The next things were the Walking Skirts for daily use. If the skirt did the walking then why wear it? The article went on to say that one must have the undergarment to match what they were purchasing. Again, I could not help wondering why anyone would wear a matching undergarment if it was to be hidden under an outer garment…quite strange these lady's clothes. It seemed to me that if humans dressed like clocks, things would be much simpler.

Finally they stopped looking and spoke to each other and Molly figured out loud,

"Let's see now, a dress for Mable Ann, waists, skirts, under skirts and corsets for the two ladies at a terribly high cost of $13.50 plus the $0.75 for Mable Ann's dress. And this didn't even include the shipping costs!

The rest of August and the first two weeks of September moved along quickly. The ladies received their clothing in early October, but nothing earth shattering was happening. It seemed as though Don was slowing down. He spent more time sitting in the parlor than he had in the past, and this was just not like the Don everyone all knew and loved.

The city elections came and went, and Mayor Maloney was in for another term. Julius was elected to the 4th Ward as Alderman and had to spend a lot more time with administration than he had planned on. The city was growing and had reached a population of 35,000 people. (12)

Don explained, "That was nothing to sneeze at when you consider the whole country only has 92,228,996 people in it."

Molly found the new library and met Miriam Huxley, the new librarian, who was quite thrilled with the new building located right across from the park. She brought home special books for Mable Ann.

One afternoon, in late September, Molly came home from the library and found Don sitting in the living room, where I had been watching him sleep.

"Hon, are you alright?"

She nudged him with her hand on his shoulder and he didn't move.

"Don, don't frighten me, are you awake?" Still, he didn't move. Hysterically she shook him and called him again, "Don, oh Don, please wake up, please wake up!"

He opened his eyes slowly, and with a faint voice, not at all like his normal one, he answered her.

"I don't feel well Molly. Maybe I have eaten something I should not have?"

Molly gently scolded him, "If you recall, both Catherine and I have suggested you should see the doctor, or try some kind of tonic."

Don was a bit belligerent, "I have never had to take anything in my life, and I don't care to start now!"

"You just sit right there. I'm going to fetch Catherine; maybe she has an idea of how to help now that you have decided you won't accept any from me."

Molly left and then returned quickly with her daughter in tow.

"Daddy, what's wrong?"

"I don't know Catherine, I don't know. I just can't seem to get up."

"I think I know something that can help. Julius's brother uses it and he says it helps him. I'll go get it, I have some at the house for when he visits and has a spell."

She left as quickly as she had appeared, then she returned again, but this time with a bottle in her hand.

Don inquired, "What is that?"

Catherine answered, "It is called Vin Vitae. Val swears by it. He gets it from the catalogue."

"You have to remember there is a considerable age difference between Val and me." Don reluctantly remarked.

"But daddy, what can it hurt?"

"Probably nothing, but I am very skeptical of these 'witch doctor' medicines."

"Now daddy, be practical. Do you think that Sears and Roebuck would sell something dangerous?"

"Being honest, yes I do. I think if they can make money on it, they will do so regardless of the product and its value."

"Well, I trust them! Just listen to what they have to say,

"You should take Vin Vitae if you answer yes to any of these questions." (13)

Now I am going to read them to you."

She hesitated and looked at him to be sure he was listening.

"Are you easily tired?"

Don nodded, "I guess so."

"Do you sleep badly?"

"No, I sleep like a top." He answered.

"Are you nervous?"

He smiled slightly, then feebly raised his finger toward them, "Only when you two gang up on me."

Catherine continued, ignoring his sarcastic remark, "Do you feel exhausted."

"That's apparent, isn't it?"

Catherine smiled this time, and then she continued.

"Have you lost your appetite?"

This time Molly answered for him.

"No he hasn't. Still eats like a horse."

Catherine grinned at her mother's answer and asked the next question that was written in the Sears and Roebuck catalogue.

"Is your stomach weak?"

Don smiled slightly, "Only when Julius drives the motor car."

"Now daddy, that wasn't nice."

"Probably not, but at least it is true."

"Okay, next question. Are you thin?"

All three stopped and slowly took a look at Don's midsection, which seemingly had grown somewhat since his retirement, and then they all decided at the same time to not answer that question, but instead, just giggle and point.

"Another one, and then I have only a couple more. Is your circulation poor?"

Molly had been berating Don for some time about his being cold all the time. There was little doubt that the circulatory problem existed.

"I can answer that one. He wears a sweater all the time these days, and when I open the bedroom window for some fresh air, he closes it. Does that answer your question?"

"Yes, it does mother. Okay, this is the last one. Are you weak, either constitutionally or from recent sickness?"

Don was showing some irritation at the questioning, and in a feeble, but disgusted voice he answered.

"I'll answer that one myself. My morning constitutional is a private affair. I can tell you my constitution and I am getting along fine. As to recent illness I haven't had any, as you both know. That is until this last week or so, that I seem to be under the weather."

It seemed to me that he had forgotten his bout with the stamina and other things that had happened to him before leaving the old home. Maybe I had just misunderstood at the time, but as I recall he had been sick.

"Now assuming it will make you both happy I'll try your Vin Vitale, but I am not in favor of it."

"Here mother, fill this spoon and give it to father," Catherine instructed.

It was interesting to watch as Molly lowered the spoon toward her husband's mouth, and the face that he made before the potion even entered into it. Of course my works could neither make faces nor complain, thank goodness.

By the end of September Don had tried all of the Sears Roebuck products, including Dr. Hammonds Nerve and Brain Pills, Wonderful Little Liver Pills, Dr. Bain's Famous Blood Pills, and Blackberry Balsam. He had said to Molly, on more than one occasion, that perhaps he had worms and should try some worm medicine like Reliable Worm Syrup. Molly said that she didn't think that would do any good, and besides, he would know if he had worms! I know that would be terrible for me because worms would eat my wooden body and make holes in it. I could only guess what they could do to Don!

"Hon, you know as well as I do something is wrong, and you need help. Let's consult a doctor."

Don thought about it for a bit, and then he answered. "Okay you are probably right, do you have the name of a good doctor handy?"

"Anna Jepsen has suggested a family friend who is also a doctor. Dr. Brown is his name. She says he is a very bright young man."

"Well, if Anna has recommended him he must be well thought of. She seems to know everyone in this place."

October the third came, a bright and clear Monday morning. The doctor looked tired for his years, but as I understand it, these doctors work long hours every day and have few hours to themselves.

I was delighted to see a new face, not realizing this was not someone you normally welcome wholeheartedly.

"Good morning. I am Doctor Brown. You called me yesterday with respect to your husband."

"Please come in."

"Don is still upstairs. We didn't expect you so early. Can I get you a cup of tea?"

"No, that won't be necessary. I have a very tight schedule today, with many calls to make. It is like an epidemic lately with ill folks. Before I see him, perhaps you can give me some details about his illness?"

Pointedly, the doctor asked, "What has he been taking for the condition?"

Molly listed the things they had purchased, and I could see that the doctor was not happy with the news.

"So you are telling me that you have allowed him to purchase that "witch doctor" medicine. Do you know that for the most part, it is just plain alcohol?"

"Alcohol, you mean we have been giving him table-spoon after table-spoon of alcohol all of this time?"

Doctor Brown looked at her sternly, and said, "Yes, I am afraid you have, along with a lot of other unproved drugs. If it makes you feel any better, you are not the first to try these home remedies."

Molly weighed her next comment carefully. "If these things are so bad why hasn't "Good Housekeeping" gotten after them?

"Oh, that they could! You see Good Housekeeping laboratories only test food products. The drug business is a huge industry to fight. They hire hundreds of people to tell you how wonderful their products are, and many of them are being made in the back yard, so to speak. Do you understand what I am trying to say?"

He continued, "Please tell me everything you can about his past, clear up to the time he started feeling ill. Can you do that?"

Molly quietly answered, "I will try."

She told him all that she could recall, from the time he was looking a bit tired in Waterbury, up until the most recent episodes. She also told him about Don's daily glass of brandy and the cigar habit that he had recently given up.

The doctor listened and made notes that could be of value in his diagnosis. How much simpler it would be were his insides like mine, made of metal and just needing a minor adjustment or perhaps some oil from time to time.

When the doctor had finished getting the information he needed, a half hour or more had gone by.

"Mrs. Holscomb, it is time for me to see our patient now. Would you direct me to his room please?"

Later Catherine and Julius, accompanied by little Mable Ann, came to visit, and to inquire about what the doctor had to say. As they sat in the parlor, Don's absence was quite noticeable. Catherine was the first to speak.

"Where is daddy? Is he confined to bed now, or something else worse?"

Molly responded reluctantly after Catherine's comment, "Doctor Brown spent most of the morning here today. First he asked me for all of the information I could remember, as to Don's health and its decline.."

Catherine interrupted, "You did tell him about the coloration didn't you mother?"

Molly answered, "Of course dear. That was very important."

Julius interceded, "Catherine, let your mother tell us. You know that she would not leave anything important out."

"I know, but it is just so exasperating to not have been here."

Now even Catherine had tears in her eyes. I had never seen the family in such turmoil. It is always difficult for me to understand ailments of any kind, with humans. When I stop working properly they take me to the clockmaker and he makes an adjustment here and there, and as I said before, then they put that liquid oil in a few places and send me home fit as a clock should be.

"It is not good. Your father has developed a bad heart along with pneumonia. It seems he has had the heart condition for some time, and all of those tonics did not do him any good, especially considering the amount of alcohol and other unknowns in them."

Catherine exclaimed, "Alcohol and unknowns?"

Molly responded, "Yes, alcohol and unknowns."

"Do you mean to tell me that Val has been taking alcohol and some other unknown substances, and his mother didn't even realize it?"

"I guess that is true. Remember though, Anna has lived through a time when all that was available were remedies, mostly homemade, so these new things, with all the publicity about them, sounded good."

"I suppose, but Anna is so solid in her judgment, I just can't believe that..."

Julius spoke up, "Mom makes mistakes, just a like anyone else, but Val has a mind of his own, and is old enough to make those health decisions. Let's not think about them right now, let's hear more about Don."

Molly continued, "The pneumonia apparently can't always be detected. There is this 'walking pneumonia' which is difficult to diagnose, someone may think it is a bad cold. Of course when it doesn't go away with ordinary means, one should contact a doctor, but few have. You know how your father dislikes being babied in any form."

"So what now mother?"

"The doctor has given orders for complete bed rest. No exercise or stressful things of any kind for at least two weeks, and definitely no more brandy or cigars. He is to stay in bed and only get up to go to the toilet, nothing else. I am to give him this new drug called aspirin, twice a day, and feed him a lot of liquids. The doctor will be back in two weeks. Of course if we need him sooner we can call him at home." (14)

The next two weeks were critical. My ticking was the only sound, except for the occasional whistle of the teapot signaling that the boiling had taken place, or the lonesome sound of the train whistle.

Every other day or so, Julius would slip around the house and into the garage out back, to start the new motor car. It seemed that he took too much pleasure in doing it, but on the other hand, like me, it needed to run.

Anna came to visit and brought along her friend, Mrs. Mortensen. Val and his wife Mae would drop in occasionally and then go next door to visit Julius and Catherine. Catherine was here every morning at a sharp 9:00 A.M. to check up on her mother, for fear she would be overdoing in her care for Don.

The parade of visitors was seemingly never to end; young Sam and his fiancée, Kathleen; the minister from the church; and there were others I was not privy to know. I had to assume most of those folks were met at the store on the corner, or perhaps at some other place the family went and left me behind sitting on my mantle.

One afternoon, Julius stopped by to visit with Don who was relaxing in the living room. Don told Julius his innermost thoughts; about the afterlife; and about his feelings about his own life. He told him about his belief in God and how that belief had always been the stalwart foundation in everything he did.

He changed the subject about his beliefs and asked Julius to take care of his car, advising him that that it needed started every day.

"I can never give into something like an illness. God is with me, and I with him, I am in a continuous prayer now to look after Molly. He knows my every thought."

"I guess, that if you have that kind of faith, it is good. I could never understand it."

"You mean that you don't have any faith?"

"Not really. I am not sure that there is a God. If there was one, why would he allow you to be sick?"

"I must say Julius, I never thought of you as a non-believer. There is a reason for everything, and it is all in the bible. Have you never read it?"

"Never. Let us just say that I believe in what I can see. I believe in what I can do. I believe in reality, not fantasy!"

Don was having difficulty with the conversation. As long as I can remember, I never heard a discussion like this one before. I knew that Don and Molly attended a church where they saw their God every Sunday, and that they prayed before every meal and assumed everyone did the same.

"I don't think you have the right attitude Julius."

Don sounded weak with his voice, but strong in his convictions.

"You could be right Don, but I'm happy the way I am. I still feel that if there was a God, He would not let fine folks like you become ill. You know I lost my father to the sea; he was a sailor in the Danish Navy. God should have looked after him because he was a God fearing man… but He didn't."

Don answered his son-in-law carefully, "I will continue to believe that whatever God does, He does with a reason. I may not understand it all, but I firmly believe, just the same that something good will come out my illness, even if I never know what that might be."

Julius disagreed, "You can believe what you wish Don, just as I do. Let's not discuss this any further and just remain the good friends that we have become, alright?"

Don dropped his eyes as he spoke, more quietly than before ."The day will come Julius, and you will understand about heaven."

CHAPTER 21

Two more weeks have passed. I heard an agonizing cry from the bedroom upstairs that echoed throughout the house. Molly was frantic as she rushed to the phone, next to the parlor door. She lifted the receiver and with an anxious voice asked for Dr. Brown. I could hear both ends of the conversation quite clearly, from where I sat on the mantle.

"This is Dr. Brown, how can I help you."

"Doctor, this is Molly Holscomb, Don's wife."

"Yes Molly, what's wrong?"

"It's Don, Doctor. He isn't breathing, can you come quickly?"

"I'll be right there Molly."

Molly hung up the phone and rushed back up the stairs. I could hear her talking loudly.

"Please Lord, don't take my Don," she sobbed. "Don, you have to breath! Please breath, the doctor is coming!"

It seemed like only minutes when the doctor came into the house, without knocking, and bounded up the stairs.

He shouted, "Molly, can you hear me?"

There was no response. I could hear Molly as she walked back and forth and her weeping made my works almost stop. What could be wrong? Was Don worse? What did Molly mean when she said, "He stopped breathing?" Is that like me stopping ticking?

I could hear the doctor and Molly come slowly down the stairway. Molly was leaning against the doctor as they came into the parlor where I sat on the mantle.

In his most soothing voice, the doctor said, "You have to be brave Molly. We knew this was going to happen. It was just his time. There, there. Here, take this handkerchief.

Molly sobbed as she spoke, "Why Doctor, why now? The holidays are coming, and he was so happy during them. He has Mable Ann to take care of, and he got that new car."

"There is no answer Molly. I wish there was something I could do, but he had too much of a heart problem before you called me. It was just too late. I am so sorry."

Molly slowed her sobs as she spoke, "Can you wait here until I tell our daughter?"

Dr. Brown pushed her away from his arm's cushioned rest, "Of course Molly. I will wait."

The date was October 30th, 1910. Don's time had come. This was the second time that this thing called death had arrived. I didn't understand, but it was much more disturbing this time than when Jim left the family. Even I, just a clock, felt the loss. Perhaps it was because Molly was here, right in front of me.

For the next few days, people came and went; some, of whom, I recognized, and others I did not. Some said he looked good, while others just looked, and then they turned away. As he laid in front of me, I studied his face, not wanting to forget it. He and Molly had always loved me so.

By the end of the week, the men came and took Don away. I have no idea where they took him, but I understood that I would never see him again.

Molly sat by the hour and looked at the fireplace. She ran her hand over his big chair. She opened and closed the door in the corner cabinet carefully, as she ran her fingers over the edge of the door.

A week passed when she got up and looked at me. "Well, old friend, I think it is time for you to have a new owner, someone who will be here long after I am gone."

I was frightened. Did she mean I was going to be sold? How could she do that, just because Don was gone; why did I have to go too?

"I know that you are just a wooden clock, but you have been a part of our family from the very beginning. It is time for you to move on now. You are lucky you don't have feelings. I know that Catherine will treasure you, just as Don and I have."

What did she mean that I didn't have feelings? If only she knew. It was then that I realized my value. What other gift could be given to Catherine and Julius that would come so much from the soul of Molly. I felt proud, even though I was very sad that I would be leaving. I suppose though, on the bright side, she will come and visit me regularly. If I could weep, I would do so about now. This was better, and yet worse than the auction, because then I could get upset, now all I had was grief.

The day had started slowly, but then a letter arrived through the post for Molly. The timing could not have been better. It is from her sister-in-law, Claudia, and she read it out loud (as she generally did) claiming she could understand the content better which was wonderful for me to be able to hear.

November 3, 1910
Dear Molly,
I know how you must feel at this time having been there myself not too awful long ago. It is with deep love for you that I write this letter of encouragement. The loss of a husband is not a good time and I found that focusing on the good times helped. We did have a lot of those didn't we?

I know I don't write often enough and for that I must apologize. While this may not be the time to tell you about the boys, I thought it might be good to think about them. I believe the last time I wrote I told you one was getting married, that would be Billy, of course, and it has happened. Mike has gone on to college and is about to graduate. I am very proud of them both.

Well, I must close for now. Please write soon and let me know how you are. I miss you greatly.

Love,

Claudia.

I watched and listened to her as she read the letter. I felt her grief. It was apparent to me that the loss of a loved one can be quite devastating for a human, and while I was incapable of such feelings, I felt as though I still felt her pain..

She went to the desk, opened the top drawer, and removed a small box. The letter was placed with other ones she had received and tied with a blue ribbon. She closed the drawer and came to where I was sitting. Molly, lifted me from my resting place on the mantle, lovingly caressed me as she might another human being, and carefully carried me through the den into the hall and out of the front door to Catherine's house next door.

"Now I know that we haven't discussed this at all, but this wonderful clock has been in our family for 31 years. It has never missed a beat and it is so perfect. I would like to give the clock to you and Julius."

"Mother," Catherine, with tears welling in her eyes answered, "you love that clock so, how could you give it up?"

"That's the point. I do love it, and your father and I thought that passing it on, while you could enjoy it, would be great; something that you could pass on later to your children. I know that is what he would have liked."

With tears of joy streaming down her face, Catherine hugged her mother.

"I am speechless! I have to sit down because this has made my legs weak, I never imagined ever, that you would do this."

"Well, it is the thing to do. I will find a smaller clock for my mantle, and you can put this special family clock on yours."

Molly turned toward the door, and with a tear in her eye, returned to her own home next door

I don't know whether I am glad or sad. Leaving Molly, and only seeing her occasionally just doesn't feel right; but I suppose I will adjust to it. Catherine is a part of my life too, but how will Julius accept me?

A new chapter in my life was beginning; there was the excitement of Mable Ann and her friends being around; the younger generation with their parties and meeting new people. It was almost too much to think about.

Catherine accepted me and laid a crocheted doily on top of the mantle before placing me there. It is as though I am on a pedestal, a thing on display.

I must admit it is a wonderful feeling. She took the key and inserted it into the holes in my face and turned it clockwise to be sure my works were wound. Next, she took a soft cloth, put a small amount of tongue oil on it, and polished my surface. I would like to have moved a bit from side to side as she massaged my body, but of course I could not. The warmth of her hands delighted me. I felt like I was at home.

CHAPTER 22

"I'm home hon: I left my job early today. Did you remember that tomorrow is your Birthday?"

"Of course I remember, it has been my birthday since 1881 and no one ever lets me forget it. Especially those that point out I am approaching middle age already."

"Middle age? That's strange, just imagine approaching middle age at this early time!"

"Yes." Catherine interrupted bluntly.

Smiling, Julius replied, "It just dawned on me, that I was born a year or so earlier than you, so that makes me really getting up there, doesn't it?"

A slight frown darkened Catherine's face as she responded, "That is frightening! Let's not talk about it anymore."

Julius turned his head and noticed me sitting on the mantle behind him.

"What's this?"

"Oh, you noticed did you?"

"Of course I noticed. It's your folk's clock. I have heard so much about its history, and I know that Don and your mother loved it so. What is it doing here?"

"Mother gave it to me."

" You don't mean...?"

"Yes I do. Can you imagine? I guess that proves that they loved us both very much.

"I can see how that says she loves you, but us?"

"Yes silly. She knows that we are going to stay together forever, and that we love each other dearly. Mother gave the clock to us knowing that we would take care of it, and guard it fearlessly and forever, or at least until it would be time for us to hand it down. Isn't that wonderful?"

Julius at last understood, "Yes it is. I can't wait for my mother to see it on our mantle. She appreciates beautiful things too. I know that the clock meant so much to your parents, and it meant so much to Don. Maybe this is what he was trying to tell me before he died. What life is all about, about love and caring."

"What are you talking about?"

"Nothing really, just a private conversation Don and I had before he left us for his heaven."

"His heaven? Isn't it our heaven too?"

Julius took her in his arms, "I think it may be... now."

It was a relief for me to hear that Julius thinks I fit into their home, and that he loves me too, I had some doubts. After all he is a cabinetmaker, a carpenter, a sign maker, an Alderman, (again, and as usual, I have no idea what Alderman means) and who knows what else? He works with beautiful wood all of the time. I imagined that he could have thought I didn't fit here.

The two of them left the parlor, hand in hand, and headed toward the kitchen. It was barely 3:30 PM and Mable Ann was just awakening from her afternoon nap. I could hear her gentle footsteps as she came down the stairs, apparently awakened by her father's voice. She looked into the den and was astonished to see me there. She was trying to understand how I could be here and at her grandmother's house at the same time. I watched her back away, quietly. I knew she was going to question her mother how this could be. I could hear her go into the kitchen and ask her mother about me.

"Mother, do we have a clock like grandma's?"

"I guess that you have been in the living room, haven't you? Doesn't the clock look pretty in there?"

"Yes it does mother, but how did we get one, just like grandma's?"

"We didn't sweetheart. That one was grandma's clock, but she gave it to me this morning."

"Will grandma give me one someday too, like that one?"

Molly smiled, "No, this was the only one that she had, and now it is ours, but someday, in the far away future, it will be yours."

Mable Ann puzzled that for a bit, then innocently asked, "Maybe next year?"

"No," Catherine answered, "not that soon. You will be married first, and have a little child, just like you, before that happens."

Then, as nonchalant as a child often can be, she left the kitchen, no longer concerned.

"Okay,"

I have discovered that the wonderful thing about children is they don't linger on things that don't affect them directly. Their minds can turn it on and off as rapidly as the wind blows. It was not how obscure their view of life seemed to be, but yet, how innocent they are, and without judgment.

I could hear the family as they chatted in the other room as clear as my gong. All that remained in my thoughts was how exciting it was going to be to see new people, and to hear new conversations!

"Catherine," Julius called from the bedroom. "Is today the day?"

It was a question that hardly needed asking. With the smell of turkey roasting, the pies being baked, the sound of pots and pans being put here and there. There was little doubt it was the day when food was the one thing you could be certain of. Even lacking a good sense of smell, the marvelous odor of food cooking came billowing from the kitchen like smoke from a train engine.

"Yes dear, today is Thanksgiving and we are going to have a lot of company; your mother; her friends, Charlie and Elsie Johnson; our friends, Sam, and his fiancée, Kathleen. Counting our mothers, you and me, and Mable Ann, we will have about nine people, and that should be enough, don't you think?"

"That sounds like a room full alright. Are we going to try to fit them all in the dining room at once?" Julius sounded concerned.

"They will fit fine. We have room for eight when I open up the round oak table and we can sit Catherine between you and me on the stool. It should work out well... I think."

"Then all of the food will be on the table too?"

"No, I am going to use the sideboard for most of it. I am sitting you next to it so that you can reach the food and send the dishes, one at a time, around the table, then place them back on the sideboard when they are returned back to you. Okay?"

Julius nodded, "You always plan things out so well."

"I learned it well from my mother."

"I see, and did Don learn to do what I will be doing now?"

Catherine smiled as she said,"Of course!"

It was good to see my new owners so enamored with each other. They are so much like Don and Molly that one would think Julius had been a family member all of his life. Maybe in spirit, he was, who knows?

"Now that everything has been decided, how soon are we going to invite the January guests?" Julius asked.

"We have plenty of time. I think we should at least let everyone get Thanksgiving and Christmas over with before we suggest another party, don't you?" Catherine replied.

"Of course you are right again. I just get a bit excited about these things. You know we are going to be hosting more people, due to my political campaigns. When I run for City Alderman again, I don't intend to lose."

"And you won't lose either, I am confident of that," Catherine agreed.

Then, as if from nowhere, a voice I have heard a million times, (that may be an exaggeration) echoed from the hall door.

"Do you need some help?" Molly asked as she entered the room.

"Mother, I thought you weren't going to show up to help." Catherine teased.

"Dear, it's only 7:30 A.M. What can I do to help?"

The day had started. Molly did everything that mothers are asked to do.

Julius reminisced, "It's times like these that I miss that old cigar odor. It just seemed to take the edge off. Of course the brandy didn't hurt either, but I guess those days are gone."

Catherine's birthday was celebrated this year along with Thanksgiving, and it went smoothly and quickly. The only discussion, other than Don's passing, or something about the Maxwell, was when Julius was asked if his friend, Sam, knew that freight was being moved by an aeroplane, or not. Of course, he said he had not, but he did know that the Wright Brothers had one flown from Dayton to Columbus by some fellow named Phillip Parmalee. (15)

I still wondered why anyone would want to be up in the air, in one of those things they so often describe as being heavier than air. Foolhardy nonsense it seems to me, but then, what do I know, I am just a wooden clock.

Finally Christmas arrived, and with it most of the gaiety of the past. This year it was different since Catherine and Julius now had the big dinner at their home.

This time there was no toast by the fireplace by Don, with his brandy in one hand, and his cigar in the other. There were none of the many family friends of the past with their laughter and gaiety.

There still was turkey with all the trimming, a fresh bottle of Betty Anne wine from the Council Bluffs Grape Growers Association, some home canned vegetables from the basement, and topped off with those wonderful pies baked by Anna, Catherine and of course, Molly. It was a gala affair, although not quite the same.

Molly and Catherine wore their dresses and blouses that had been recently purchased from the Sears catalogue and Mable Ann was decked out in her new dress purchased at the same time, last August.

Anna continued to be the drab one, in her homemade dress. She could not understand why anyone would throw away their hard earned money on something that any woman, 'worth her salt,'(as she would say) could make at home.

Val came with Mae, who of course had to dress in the highest fashion of the time for the occasion. She was wearing a hat with a long white feather adorning its wide brim and decorated with smaller feathers around the edges. In the center of her dress, a beautiful broach adorned her throat. The dress had long silken black sleeves, with white lace around each wrist. It ended just above her ankles and it gave a slendering appearance to her body. There was a beautiful pin that had features I could not make out, but the brilliance of it suggested jewels of some kind.

Val came dressed neatly, as always. His gray suit, with the top button fastened, and leaving the rest of the coat open to expose his vest where his gold watch chain crossed from one side to the other. His bow tie was black, and tied neatly. His glasses were tucked tightly against the bridge of his nose but they didn't distract from his handsome features.

It was strictly a family affair;, the men eating, the gossip thriving, and wine never ending. Unlike the times before, there was no after dinner cigar, or brandy glasses being sought to fill for the men. Somehow it just didn't seem the same as before.

Still, it was a pleasant day and evening, and no one mentioned the absence of Don, but I felt that I could see him there among the men.

CHAPTER 23

The new year seems to arrive so quickly after the Christmas festivities but I am always anxious for the January 10th party to take place. Although it seemed a bit too close to Mable Ann's January 7th birthday, I overheard that the plan is to make one party instead of two. They would celebrate Mable Ann's, during the day of the 10th, and the other party during the evening of the 10th.

There will be new faces, new conversations, new world events! I know that for a clock to be so excited is perhaps foolish. On the other hand, how else is a clock going to learn, except by being stationed in a perfect place, where I have been for so long, and hearing whatever is being said? (Of course there is also that box that talks.)

"Are you as excited as I am Julius?" Catherine inquired.

"Yes I am. I know that your Mother is looking forward to this as much as we are, and no doubt so is mine."

"I am sure you are right about that. Do you think we have forgotten anyone?"

Julius looked discouraged. "I don't see how. We have gone over this a dozen times, but if it will make you feel any better, we can check one more time?"

Catherine's face flushed. "Of course, you are right. We don't need to do that again, I think I am just nervous... aren't you?"

Julius felt the need to placate his loving wife. "Tell you what, I will read off the names, you check them off mentally, and that way we will both be sure we have not forgotten anyone, okay?"

"Okay, read on." Catherine smiled.

"Let's start with the easy ones."

Julius picked up the list from the desk and started reading.

"My mom, your mother, Uncle Val and Aunt Mae, Sam and Kathleen, mom's friends Elsie and Charlie Johnson, your friend Maude Walters, Ed Nelson, the fire chief, Mr. and Mrs. Rasmussen from across the street, Mr. and Mrs. Mortensen from the grocery store, General Dodge," he stopped short of the next one, then asked, "and that inventor fellow, the one I told you about last week, you remember don't you?"

"I'm not sure honey. You meet so many people at the court house."

"He was born here in Council Bluffs in 1873. He just came back to look for the location of some past relatives at the cemetery.

I believe he said… oh yes, now I recall his name, it was Lee DeForest."

"But if you just met him, why would you invite him, a total stranger to the party?"

"Do you remember all of the important and interesting folks your dad used to invite to his parties?"

"Yes I do, but he knew them all."

"I know, but this fellow seemingly knows no one here, and will only be around for a week or so. He's quite alone."

"Okay, we'll invite him. What's one more anyway? Maybe, he will be a good conversationalist."

"Okay I am adding him. That will make eighteen, including us; that is, if everyone shows up. Incidentally speaking of showing up, have you heard from the General?"

"No, and I don't think that he called mother back either. Maybe I should call him?"

"Let's just leave it. If he comes, he comes, and if he don't…,well he just don't. He probably has a lot on his mind, or perhaps he didn't even come back from New York as he had planned."

While all of this conversation was going on, I wondered if this would be as much fun as the parties of old. I wondered if the General would return the call but there was no way I would know unless I was to overhear a conversation on the telephone. Really, I should not be concerned.

*I imagined hearing Molly amusing herself,
while standing in front of her bedroom mirror.*

"I think I will wear one of my better
dresses, put a ribbon in my hair, with one of the
fancy hair pins I have. I have those nice new
shoes and I will match the color of my dress."

*She would hesitate and then point a finger at
her reflection in the mirror.*

"Now if you get too gussied up,
too many of these gentlemen may turn out to be
not 'too gentlemanly,' we are in the West you
know. It would be nice if you meant that. You
are being bad aren't you?"

*She would try to joke herself into believing
that she would not miss her wonderful Don but I
knew that she could not dismiss her deep down
thoughts.*

*Sam and Kathleen had talked about becoming
man and wife on several occasions, and while quite
serious about each other, they had never talked about
their differences before. For some reason they arrived
early for the party, and while waiting for their hosts
to become readied, I overheard their rather interesting
discussion. Kathleen started, while looking into Sam's
dark brown eyes.*

"You know, we come from different life
styles, different religions...does this bother you?

Sam thought for a moment, then
answered, "Yes, at times."

"Just at times?" Kathleen countered.

Sheepishly, Sam answered, "Well kind of."

"What I am trying to say is that you don't understand what makes my life complete, do you?"

"I thought I did, until now. Does that mean that you don't really understand me?"

"Let's examine this a bit." Kathleen, who rarely had much to say, seemed concerned about the final step they were contemplating. "I like to do things with other folks. I like fondue, I like special dinners with people, and I like music. What do you like?

"I guess I like music too, although I don't know one note from another, so whatever you call music may or may not really fascinate me as much as it could.

I like people too, but I have to tolerate them at work all day long. Now that doesn't mean I would not enjoy them at a meal, but I like us being alone."

Katherine explained, "I didn't mean I want people I hardly know. I like to talk to our friends during dinner, discuss events, things, or whatever. Wouldn't you like to have Julius and Catherine over for a dinner, after we get married?

"I could accept that."

Kathleen seemed almost out of patience when she replied, "You say that you understand that, but why can't we enjoy other people during a meal too? You know, for instance, having folks you don't have to work with every day, but that you might like to know better.

It might be good to learn about the way others live, or to discuss new things that we don't normally talk about?

Sam responded with, "You don't mean pry into their life do you?"

"Of course not silly, you can have nice conversations without prying into some else's affair."

She hesitated for a second, and then she asked, "Okay, maybe we will only do casual conversation and no dinners. There can't be anything wrong with that is there? We have nothing in our private lives that we have to be secretive about, is there?"

Sam answered, "Everything; our life, our marriage, our thoughts, our religious situation....those things are all private."

Kathleen seemed relentless in her prodding for Sam's thoughts.

"Okay. Let's assume our lives are private. Does that mean that we can't have a fun meal in front of the fireplace, maybe a glass of wine, just a nice quiet and casual evening? We don't have to tell everything, especially since you believe that our life should be so secretive!"

"I think that how we live, where we are on the income scale, what we do, or have done ...those things are all personal."

"I guess then, that maybe the best thing is for us to just settle down in our house, lock the doors, never answer the phone and live like some recluse...would that be right?"

Sam, realizing that he was alienating his Irish colleen, softened his abrupt answers.

"You are right. I am being pig headed. I don't believe that it's anyone's business how we live, but let's just continue to be happy, live a quiet life, have some folks that we both like come once in a while, and let things take their course. We are happy, aren't we?

I watched as Kathleen withdrew into her thoughts. I could understand that she wanted them to be happy. I thought that the religious aspect I had heard about before might come further to the surface, but it didn't. It appeared to me that she felt it best to say no more. Another time, another place perhaps, all that mattered now was their happiness.

It seemed terribly quiet after that. A knock sounded from the door, breaking the silence,. The Rasmussens from across the street had arrived to help Catherine and Julius dashed down the stairs to let them in.

Julius and Hans had a lot in common as they did house repair, cabinet work and updating homes, together in many cases; and Bess was a friend of Catherine's, much like Margaret and Molly had been.

"Welcome, and do come in. My goodness Bess, you do look marvelous, as usual of course. I didn't catch you before you left earlier to tell you how much your help in the preparation of this party is appreciated." Julius turned to his friend and working partner, "And you, Hans, you just get uglier every day."

Hans's burly voice resonated in his answer, "Thanks so much, you damn Dane."

Bess intervened, "Now look you two, keep your compliments about each other to yourselves; let's not ruin Catherine's party!"

Julius had no sooner escorted his first guests to the living room when the knocker broke the silence of the hall once again.

"I'll get it sweetheart."

Julius rushed back down the hall and opened the front door. There he found his brother and sister-in-law waiting. "Welcome Val and Mae. You are the third to arrive. Please come in."

Mae, with her usual ungrateful attitude, inserted her uppity sentiment, "Thank you. We have brought mother with us, since we felt that we were early, so that she did not have to walk over here alone."

Julius refrained from 'dressing down' his sister-in-law. "Thanks for that, I was just getting ready to go after her when Hans and Bess arrived."

He ushered them all in, then turned to Anna, and kissed her on the cheek.

"Hello mother, and how are you tonight?"

Anna, disregarding his kiss, answered in her, usual harsh voice.

"Quite well, thank you! I am glad I didn't wait for you!"

"Now listen you two," Val intervened with a smile on his face. "do I have to be your mediator?"

The four of them came into the living room where Hans had been talking to Sam and Kathleen. I could see that they were smiling. I was afraid that the evening was going to be starting off badly for Julius and Catherine, but it appears as though the disgust was all in jest, well most of it anyway. Anna sat on the stool next to the couch. It was a cute little sewing stool that seemed to fit her rounded behind quite well. It had four spindled legs, each attached to a corner of the 'bowl shaped' seat. The cross-members that stretched between the legs had what appeared to be plant root, but it was probably some kind of heavy cord wound about them, and then sealed into place.

Val and his wife sat on the two-seater placed at the other end of the couch leaving the couch itself for a group of three, should there be a need. No sooner had everyone sat down, and Julius started to leave the room, than the doorknocker sounded once again and I could hear Julius as he welcomed his guests. "Ah, Mr. Mortensen and Mrs. Mortensen, how nice of you to come, please do come in.

I could hear him take their wraps, and place them on the bench in the entry hall.

"Please follow me."

"Thank you Julius."

He and his wife followed him, but before they entered into the living room, Mrs. Mortensen pointed her finger close to her husband's nose.

"Now Morton, be on your good behavior, be kind to Julius and his guests or I am sure that Anna will make your life miserable, come tomorrow!"

They rounded the corner and came through the doorway of the living room just as Anna said her greeting.

"I must say Morton, it is nice to see you haven't imbibed yet." She came straight to the point with her comment.

"Now Anna, don't you start in on me. I may have had a swallow, or two, but nothing more." With that he whipped out a cigar.

His wife was quick to attack. "Morton, put that thing away. You must know that certain people aren't around, quite possibly due to smoking those foul things."

I didn't particularly like the reference to Don. It was good that Molly had not arrived yet, for surely she would have taken exception to the sarcastic remark.

"I wish you women would stop poking at us menfolk for a minute at least. Just pick, pick, pick, for goodness sake, can't a man enjoy his vices at all these days?"

I could see this could become a very interesting evening. I had not met this Mr. Mortensen before, although I had heard him shouting from time to time and remembered his uncalled for comments about Don's new Maxwell. I had also not met his wife, although I had heard her admonish him. What a great night this was going to be!

Molly's voice echoed down the hall. Apparently she had opened the door a crack, just to ask the question before entering, but fully aware that the guests were arriving.

"Hello, anyone home?"

"No one here, but us chickens," came the reply. "Come on in anyhow."

Julius jumped to his feet, and almost collided with Catherine, as she was already in route down the hall toward the door.

"Goodness Julius, I didn't know you were there!"

"Nor I you, hon, what a collision we could have had!"

He looked down and realized that he had almost run over his little daughter as well. As the three of them walked toward the kitchen door, they almost collided with Molly as she came through it.

Don became flustered in his efforts to be the gentleman he opted to be. "We are so sorry Molly, please excuse our clumsiness."

Molly answered, "Don't fret. How could I be upset? It's a wonderful change to be here and not have all of the work to do. I did bring some dessert though."

The four of them returned through the hallway, and as Julius stepped into the parlor, he pulled his pocket watch from his vest and looked at it. It apparently told him what he wanted to know, although he could have just looked at me. I am always accurate…at least I think so.

"You are all quite punctual. It is precisely 7:00 PM according to my railroad watch." He tapped the face of his pocket watch to make the point.

Julius went to the corner cabinet, and asked if anyone would like a glass of wine. Of course the ladies restrained themselves from the alcohol, but the men seemed rather fond of the idea.

He filled the five glasses with wine, and gave one to each of the men and kept one for himself. He then asked if there would be anything he could get for the ladies. They answered "No, but thank you."

It seemed but seconds after the wine had been poured, and before the men could drink from their glasses, that the door- knocker sounded once again. Julius put his glass on the mantle next to me and left the room as Molly, Catherine, and little Mable took the three seats available on the couch.

A new voice resonated from the front doorway.

"Is this the Johnson residence?"

"Yes it is. And who are…?"

"You have forgotten? You and I met briefly the other day, and you invited me to stop by this evening. This is the correct night, is it not?"

Embarrassed by his not recognizing his guest, Julius quickly responded, "Yes of course Dr. DeForest, please come in, we are all getting acquainted in the living room, let me have your coat and hat."

I could hear the coat being placed in the hall closet, and bold footsteps coming through the hall. I was very impressed with this new face. The man appeared to me to be around forty years of age, quite straight with thinning brown hair that seemed somewhat heavier on the left than on the right. He had a serious expression on his face. As he entered the room, the serious expression turned into a pleasant smile and Julius introduced Mr. Lee DeForest. He stretched his hand out to shake hands with the gentlemen that were present, one at a time.

"I recognize that name don't I?" Morton asked.

"You may sir, you may. I was born here in 1873"

Morton interrupted, "I don't think that is the reason. Did I not read about you, in our retailer's newsletter not long ago? Something about a Hertzian Wave, or something like that?"

"I see you are a well-read man sir. I did write a dissertation titled, "The Reflection of Hertzian Waves at the end of Parallel Wires."

(16)

Morton cleared his throat, "Now you have me. You could be talking Greek and I would be the lesser for the understanding. It is plain to see that you are a learned scientist."

"You are too kind. This is simply a scientific way of describing the vacuum tube. It could change the way we look at the future of radio."

Morton again spoke up, "Now I remember, you were born here, in Iowa. I read that your father was a minister, who moved about a bit, and you grew up in Talladega, Alabama."

"Again, that is correct. This is almost too embarrassing. You know all about me, and I know nothing about you."

Julius intervened, "I beg your forgiveness Dr. DeForest. It is Doctor, is it not?"

"Yes I am afraid it is. But for tonight, why not forget all of that, and just call me Lee.

That would make me much more comfortable."

Morton looked at his neighbor hoping for reinforcement.

"We would be quite happy to do that, right Julius?"

Julius took command, "Indeed, let's start the introductions. This is Morton our grocer and neighbor," then Julius turned to Val, "this is my brother Val, who works with the United States Post Office." He spun on his heel and pointed to the corner, "This is my neighbor and working partner, Hans, and this is my friend Sam, and his fiancée, Kathleen, and, as you already know, I am Julius, a carpenter and the Alderman for this, the 34th district."

Lee relaxed. "This is wonderful, now I feel like a part of the group. You have no idea how nice it is to just be a person, rather than some phenomena or worse, some rarity of mankind."

The evening was just getting settled when another voice broke through the hallway's silence.

"Julius, are we welcome when we are late?"

Before Julius could answer, the voice continued softly, as though not wanting anyone to hear.

"I know that Julius lets you smoke on the porch Charlie, but not tonight. You had best just take the pipe to the wagon, and wipe that tobacco from your lip."

I wondered who in the world was speaking. The fragrance of his pipe drifted through the air and I wondered who this person was, and if he was even invited? Then I remembered their names, the only ones not accounted for, Anna's friends, Charlie and Elsie Johnson.

Julius stood as they entered the living room. "Come on in" then he continued, "Charlie and Elsie, you know the Mortensens, and of course you know the rest of us, but you have not met Mr. DeForest, ah… rather Lee. I don't believe that you have met my mother-in-law, Molly Holscomb either."

Charlie and Elsie were formally introduced. They handed Catherine a package and that was when I discovered that each couple had brought a bread and butter gift; even Lee DeForest brought one, which I thought was a magnificent gesture. Finally everyone was accounted for. Julius was now in command, as Don used to be, and the evening was about to begin. All of the men, except Charlie, had a glass of the wine from the Council Bluffs Grape Growers Association, but that was soon rectified.

"It would be my pleasure this evening to raise a toast to our guests of honor. Do you all have a glass, with something you deem appropriate for a toast, in it?"

The women had turned down a glass before, but now, for this toast it was a necessity to have a bit of wine. Each received a glass, partially filled, before · *the toast would start. Everyone waited with great anticipation for Julius to continue.*

"We are indeed fortunate to have my mother-in-law here tonight. She moved here from Connecticut last spring," he paused and raised his glass toward his mother-in-law.

Molly stood and bowed her head slightly, embarrassed at the introduction.

Next, he turned as he held his glass high and re-introduced Lee DeForest, touting his credentials, and suggesting once again, that he just be called Lee.

With that said, he held his glass up a third time and tapped it gently with his fingernail, and then he clearly voiced the "Hear, hear" that was a tribute to Don's toasts of the past. What a grand thing to see. Each person with their glass held high.

"I raise my glass to the good health of one and all, and especially to my mother-in-law Molly, my mother Anna, and to our special guest, Lee. Skoal"

The grand toast was over and I could see a tear in Molly's eye, and as I looked around the room, a tear fell upon Catherine's cheek as well. I suspicioned that they both were reminded of Don's many toasts of the past.

"Speech, speech," everyone cried out, "we want to hear from Lee DeForest."

Lee stood, and stepped over to the fireplace next to Julius. He motioned with his hands for everyone to sit, then he said a short thank you.

"First, I don't know that I deserve such a fine toast, but of course, I will accept it graciously on behalf of these lovely ladies, Mrs. Holscomb, Mrs. Jepson and last of course, myself. I am humbled by their dignity, and pleased to be just a simple instrument of God. He has given me the knowledge, and I hope, that what I have achieved will be the beginning of a new era. We really should have raised our glasses to Julius and his marvelous wife, who worked to make this evening so memorable, so let us do that please."

Everyone remained silent for a few seconds, as though in awe of the eloquence of his words. The ladies set aside their wine glasses and sipped their tea and lemonade and the men their wine. Finally Julius stood and gave accolades to the rest of his company.

Catherine spoke up, "It is wonderful having all of you here. As most of you know, Julius's mother came all the way from Denmark, the furthest to travel those many years ago. Our friends, Sam and his lovely bride to be, Kathleen, have not traveled far, but Sam is constantly traveling up the company ladder as an 'up and coming' architect.

Sam interrupted, "Now don't butter the bread too thickly Catherine. You are starting to sound like Julius. I have only been there a little over a year, and have only designed one building."

"Yes, we know, but it is a well-known one, the Independent Order of Odd Fellows building."

Everyone clapped politely as Sam's reddened face displayed his discomfort. His embarrassment at being bragged about so profusely in front of folks he hardly knew, especially people like the distinguished Dr. DeForest, was evident.

Julius, however, paid little attention to his friend's discomfort and turned toward the Mortensens and continued on.

"Mr. And Mrs. Mortensen have built their grocery store, from a small butcher shop and handy store, into what it is today. I would venture to say everyone that lives this side of the railroad property, purchases their groceries there."

Morton could not remain quiet, as a gentleman should have. Instead of accepting the compliment, he felt it was his responsibility to embellish it a bit as he stumbled to his feet. His poor wife was embarrassed to a point of tears.
Julius continued with an attempt to speak louder than Morton, almost to a point of being rude to his neighbor.

Edith tried to quiet Morton, "You know how you get."

Julius kept increasing the volume of his speech while watching Mr. Mortensen out of the corner of his eye.

"I would be quite remiss if I were to overlook my valiant brother Val, since his station in life may soon move up to the position of Post Master for Pottawattamie County."

Val, always the gentleman, smiled and nodded his head while his wife, not nearly as gracious as he, stood and made a fool of herself, while rising to perform a poorly performed curtsy.

Julius continued, "Then, of course, there are the Rasmussens. Hans is one of the finest cabinetmakers in the county, and lives right here on our street, with his wife, Bess. She is one of the best cooks around and is also a very close friend of my lovely wife, Catherine. I might add that she was a great help in making this night possible."

Following Val's lead, Hans merely nodded, and his lovely Bess bowed her head.

"Last, but by no means least, I'd like you to meet Charlie Johnson and his wife Elsie. They are some of the finest gardeners among us. They have been in charge of the local nursery's gardens, across from the cemetery, for several years now."

Charlie was very bashful and turned away from the group, but Elsie, a large woman and generally quite stern, smiled brightly. She turned toward Charlie and lovingly touched his shoulder, then she looked at the group and thanked Julius for his remarks.

"I know Charlie won't say anything, because he never does, but Julius that was the nicest thing anyone has ever said about us. Thank you."

Without further introductions, the people all seemed to start talking at once. It was difficult for me to pick out any particular conversation, but I did overhear that Mr. DeForest would be leaving and returning to a company called Westinghouse in Chicago where he would be working on something that would make pictures move.

I assume that what I heard was true, and I wondered why can't they do the same for me?

Sam and Kathleen just looked at each other admiringly, like young lovers often do. The earlier discussions had, at least for the time being, subsided. Coyly, they tried to answer questions about their upcoming nuptials without giving a date, and without being too secretive, even though that might have pleased Sam much more.

Mr. and Mrs. Rasmussen were questioned about the work that he did; if they had any children; are there any new recipes that the ladies should know about. There were a lot questions that sounded like prying to me.

Julius and Catherine continued to circulate about the room speaking to this one, and then that one, making everyone feel more comfortable.

Anna joined Molly, being sure the "goodies," as they put it, were not going to waste, but rather consumed by the guests.

The evening wore on, as they always do, and then someone yawned, which was the beginning of the end of the delightful affair. It was at this time that I wished, in my own way, that humans could be tireless like we clocks, and just continue on.

Soon everyone left except Molly. Julius poured a bit of lemonade into Catherine's glass. He turned to Molly, who covered her glass with her hand, and shook her head back and forth in a "not for me" gesture.

"I hope that you had a good time tonight?" Julius asked as he sat back down.

Molly answered, "It was wonderful. Your friends are most gracious, and bringing in such a celebrity as Lee DeForest must have taken extreme effort on your part. What a treat for all of us."

Julius and Catherine arose with Molly, and they walked with her through the kitchen. I heard the side door open and the shuffling of her wrap as she donned it then the door closed. Julius and Catherine came back, hand in hand, and up the stairs to their private place. A perfect evening, a tired couple, a cozy bed...

CHAPTER 24

1911 had all the earmarks of becoming a good year. While Julius did not immediately change his opinion of religion, he did go occasionally to the Bethany Presbyterian Church with Catherine and little Mable Ann. I didn't know whether that was due to Don's conversation with him, or just the fact that Don's faith in his God bore fruit. Either way it was a good thing to see.

One morning Molly told Catherine that she had good news. She told her that she had invited Claudia, some time ago, to come and live with her since they were both getting up in years and were both widows. She said that she had awakened early one morning , had a small breakfast and as she was standing and looking toward the garage in the rear of the house she suddenly realized that she was lonely.

She left the kitchen and went up the stairs to

her bedroom. Still feeling as though she needed to do something she came down and went into the den. It was there that she retrieved a small group of papers from the desk drawer that were tied in a blue ribbon. She said that she untied the bow and removed the letter that was on the top of the stack and she read it to herself aloud.

September, 1909

Dear Molly,
I know how you must feel at this time having been there myself not too awful long ago. It is with deep love for you that I write this letter of encouragement. The loss of a husband is not a good time and I found that focusing on the good times helped. We did have a lot of those didn't we?
I know I don't write often enough and for that I must apologize.

It was at that point, that she got up from the big chair that Don loved so much, and went into the hallway where the phone was hung.

She picked up the receiver and asked Jenny to give her Glendale 5874 in Massachusetts.

Apparently, the phone was answered on the other end.

"Claudia? I was just reading one of your last letters and I know this is a sudden thought, but you know this house is pretty big for me. All I do is rattle around in it and wish I had some company other than the kids, at least some of the time."

There was a pause, before Claudia answered, and although I could not hear her answer, I could judge what she must have said from Molly's answer.

"You have the same problem do you? Well, why don't we just do something about it? Since your boys are on their own now, and my family is here, and Catherine speaks of missing you so often, why don't you come and share this place with me? It would be so wonderful to have you close by. We are certainly not getting any younger you know."

The family, including me, was thrilled at the prospect of Claudia coming. No date was set, but the family rejoiced knowing what was going to happen. Time passed and the incident she related was forgotten for the time being.

The wintery cold was around them all and the March winds whipped the corners of the house. I could hear Catherine humming as she worked in the kitchen. It was not unusual for her to be happy, but she had been humming for longer than usual. I heard Julius coming down the stairs, and I could tell he was listening because of the carefully made, one step at a time, quiet steps.

"Good morning sweetheart," Julius cheerfully addressed her. "Something sure smells good down here, and your humming is pretty too."

Catherine answered sarcastically and without reference to the humming.

"As if you didn't recognize the smell of ham and eggs and hash browns."

"Why are you so happy today?" Julius asked.

"Today is the day before a very important new holiday."

Catherine toyed with Julius, knowing all the time that he really knew what the day was.

"Really, and what would that be."

Julius innocently asked.

"You know very well what tomorrow is."

"No, I don't think I do. What is it?"

"It is the very first Women's Day. I know that you knew that."

"March 7th is it? Certainly you are not referring to that non-existent holiday, you do realize that it is not really a legal holiday, don't you?

"What do you mean, it isn't really a legal holiday? Your mother said it was!"

"Ah yes, but your father said it was not."

The fencing of words was escalating about this "Women's Day" thing. He left the kitchen, came into the parlor and pulled a book from the shelf, thumbed through it, then sighed what appeared to be a sigh of relief.

He returned to the kitchen with the book just as I heard Catherine finish putting breakfast on the table.

"Dear Lord," Catherine began the morning prayer," let us be thankful for all that Thou has given to us, and let us be also thankful for this food that has been prepared from the bountifulness that You have given us. We also thank You for watching over our mothers. Amen"

"That was nice Catherine. Now, let's talk about this holiday. What proof do you have that it is one?"

Without waiting for an answer, Julius opened the book he had just retrieved and read to her.

"Started as a Socialist political event, the holiday blended in the culture of many countries, primarily Eastern Europe, Russia, and the former Soviet bloc."

Catherine interrupted, "It doesn't say that we don't celebrate it here though, does it?"

Julius looked across the table, put his finger to his lips in a silencing movement, and continued reading, "In New York City, Julia Ward Howe led a "Mother's Day" anti-war observance on June 2, 1872.

Wasn't that your dad's birthday?"

"Yes it was, but I doubt that father's birthday was a time of celebration for mothers."

He continued, "Which was accompanied by a Mother's Day Proclamation. The observance continued in Boston for about 10 years under Howe's personal sponsorship, then died out."

"So now you are telling me it isn't about women, it is only about mothers! I'm a mother, aren't I. And on top of that you say that Mother's Day died out?"

Julius once again quieted her with his finger in a "shush" motion.

"Several years later, a Mother's Day observance on May 13, 1877 was held in Albion, Michigan. Frank E. Hering, President of the Fraternal Order of Eagles, made the first known public plea for "a national day to honor our mothers" in 1904, the first "official" service was on May 10, 1908. The date was declared an official holiday, but only by the state of West Virginia in 1910."

This time she interacted a bit more stubbornly.

"Then it is a holiday, is it not?" (17)

Julius laid the book aside, then he smiled at her.

"It is, in some states. I think every day is Mother's Day, because you are the most important person in the world to me, and to Mable Ann."

Catherine beamed, "You always end up saying the right thing. Maybe someday they will have a day for fathers.

Although I was not in the kitchen to see their expressions, I envisioned Julius reaching across the table to touch his wife's hand, while he smiled that loving smile of his as he looked into her eyes.

There were many happenings during the year, and all of them enlightening to me. The most wonderful of them all was the appearance of Claudia on Molly's front porch on that wonderful spring day in May. It was a surprise to all of us, except perhaps for Molly who knew right down to the hour when she was to arrive.

Julius came home early that day, and was surprised to find that Aunt Claudia had arrived so soon.

"This calls for a celebration."

Catherine nodded her agreement.

"Do you think we can get our group together hon?"

"I feel confident it can be arranged. How long ago did she arrive?"

"A couple of hours ago, and it was such a surprise. I was standing in the back yard hanging up clothes when I saw a lady approach mother's porch. All at once I realized it was Aunt Claudia. I bolted across the lawn and almost fell down on the way I was so excited. You know we have not seen her since our wedding."

The Rasmussens, the Mortensens, both of the Nelsons, the Johnsons and of course the family from Missouri Valley, Val and Mae, as well as mother Anna were assembled and the celebration began the next evening. With the normal social amenities taken care of the conversations began in the parlor, and this time they were more interesting than they had been in some time.

"I heard that while I was on the train, the city of Bangor was all but destroyed by fire."

"Really?" Everyone seemed to say at the same time.

Then a quiet and small voice asked, "Where is Bangor Aunt Claudia?"

"Bangor is in Maine, a state far, far away from here, near the Atlantic Ocean."

"I wonder if I will ever see the ocean. All I see here is the old muddy Missouri River."

Ed Nelson changed the subject.

"Did you know that the government has decided the Standard Oil Company is too large and they have designated it a monopoly?" (18)

Morton responded, "Can't keep its nose out of business can it? Damned government will probably want to own or control everything someday, gets worse right along."

Sam no doubt thought it best to change from the world of politics to something less depressing, so he brought up car racing.

"There is a new race coming up next month, has anyone heard about the Indianapolis Care Race? I understand a fellow Ray Harroun is going to drive a car named the Wasp."

It seemed as though no one had heard of the race yet. I was lost completely when he said the fellow was driving a Wasp. I also thought of them as insects and certainly not large enough for a man to mount and force his wishes upon. (19)

Sam continued, "Tell me then, have you heard of the new motor car company, something called Chevrolet? Some folks seem to think it will make old Henry Ford worry."

No one seemed aware of the goings on in the country lately, still everyone at the celebration brought up something new. The hours passed, and everyone enjoyed meeting Claudia. As each family retreated to their own home, Molly and Claudia also returned to Molly's place, exhausted but delighted with Claudia making new friends, and their renewed companionship to fill the void they both had endured.

The year moved ahead and there were many other interesting events that happened In August 1911, the painting Mona Lisa was stolen by Vincenzo Peruggis who apparently liked it too much. I will never understand what these humans find so exciting about a piece of paper, with something drawn on it. At least I contribute something of value each day, and would prefer not to have a bunch of people just standing around and staring at me! (20)

That Orville Wright fellow has been at it again. Flying in the big box with wings seems so ridiculous to me. I guess this time he stayed up in the air for nine minutes and forty-five seconds. They called the thing a glider. I can't help but wonder, what happens if it doesn't glide?

Before anyone realized it, November 12 of 1911 had arrived. Julius decided that they should celebrate Catherine's birthday in style. They talked about a guest list, what they should have for food and who would help with the work. Catherine had always relied upon her mother, her mother-in-law, and Bess, her friend from across the street to help. Now Claudia was available as well. Really, there were almost too many cooks in the kitchen. Thankfully Mae lived too far away to be helpful in the work of planning a party and Anna, bless her heart, would be able to stand for only so long before having to lie down.

Catherine swung her head toward Molly, "Mother."

Both her mother and her mother-in-law answered in unison.

"Yes dear."

Perplexed, she continued, "Oh dear, I will have to differentiate between you two won't I?"

Anna suggested. "From now on, since there are two of us, why don't you call me Anna, and your mother, mother?"

"But it sounds so ...well, so forward." Catherine cautiously replied.

Anna responded sharply, "Don't let that get in your way. I have requested it, and that's that."

Bess whispered in Catherine's ear, "I have that same situation and I use my mother-in-law's first name too. It seemed a little awkward at first, but we all got used to it."

The agreement on names was made and the ladies sat quietly for a while, drinking their tea and enjoying the marvelous cookies Anna had just baked that morning.

Catherine felt guilty planning her own birthday party. It seemed it would have been much better had someone else done it. It seemed self-serving, and she didn't particularly like the feeling.

Bess broke the silence, "Which birthday is this, or should I ask?"

Catherine blushed at the question as her mother, without giving it a second thought answered, "She'll be thirty this year."

"Really mother," Catherine said rather annoyed, "Ladies don't discuss age, or weight."

Molly reacted with an indignant, "Well, pardon me for living."

"I'm sorry mother, I didn't mean to upset you, it's just that..."

"You didn't upset me...it was supposed to be funny, but I see that there was no humor in it, I'm sorry."

Soon the big day arrived. Only the relatives, plus Bess and Hans, were invited. Julius had been quite secretive for some time. He stayed at his job later than usual on several occasions, and left on several mornings quite early, sometimes catching the morning sun as it rose above the little Missouri River town. His plans for this thirtieth birthday were special, and he had to handle it alone.

Molly arrived first, and with the old happiness in her voice, she greeted her daughter.

"Happy Birthday sweetheart, how does it feel to be out of the twenties?"

"I don't feel any different mother, should I?" Then with an afterthought she pleaded, "And please don't mention the years anymore?"

Molly smiled with her devilish grin, "I promise."

"Do you think I look older?" Catherine inquired.

Again, Molly smiled, "Of course not dear, you look the same as always... beautiful."

Catherine inquired, "Isn't it nice to have Aunt Claudia here?"

Molly took her daughter's hands in her's, and looked into her eyes, then answered, "Claudia is thrilled to be here honey. She told me that she wished she had come here with us, instead of going to her home town."

Catherine responded with, "I never knew."

Molly apologetically informed her. "I never told you."

The month always went by too quickly, with Thanksgiving on the tale end of Catherine's birthday. Then, with Christmas arriving in December followed by New Year, Molly felt fortunate that Mable Ann's birthday ended the party season and the rest of the year, until June would be less taxing.

Unlike last year, when Mable Ann's birthday was almost lost because of the big party of the 10th, her big day will be celebrated this year on January 7! I knew I would be excited and hopefully see some new faces. I overheard that Mr. Ed Nelson and his wife, Priscilla, would be coming and I wondered if he was any relation to Sam Nelson; then there was Maude Walters, Catherine's friend from childhood that had moved to Avoca, Iowa; Sam Nelson and his fiancée, Kathleen, who were Godparents to Mable.

The mayor, Thomas Maloney had been considered, but then Julius and Catherine both agreed that might make the party too political, and there was plenty of time for that nonsense. Mable Ann's friends were, for the most part, sons and daughters of the adults invited. The exception was her very best friend and classmate, Letha Wadly.

The family was dressed in their Sunday best as they sat in the living room anticipating the first arrival of their first guests. They did not have to wait long before Julius found himself greeting Sam and Kathleen.

"Good evening. Here let me take your coats."

"Thanks Julius."

Sam helped Kathleen off with her coat and handed his and her's to him as he peered around the corner. "

Are we the first ones here?"

He and Kathleen practically leaped into the living room and spoke quite loudly and in unison.

"Happy Birthday Mable Ann."

Catherine stood and greeted them as they seemed to bounce in. Sam handed Mable Ann the gift that he had been hiding behind his back.

"Oh, thank you so much."

She was excited as she retreated to her chair, the one next to the fireplace and the corner cabinet. The one her father had vacated for this special event.

The doorknocker sounded once again and this time the fire chief and his wife arrived. As Julius opened the door, he jokingly asked Ed about Priscilla, and their little daughter, Joan.

"Good afternoon Ed, and who are these beautiful ladies?"

Continuing the ruse, Ed answered, "I just found them down the street a bit, and they asked if they could come with me. How could I turn them down?"

"Oh daddy, you know that isn't true."

Julius gave Priscilla a peck on the cheek, and then he patted Joan on the head. He sat down on one knee, and looked directly at Ed's little daughter.

"Are you excited Joan?

Joan looked at him and timidly replied, "Yes sir, I sure am."

Julius smiled at her, "We are glad that you here for Mable Ann's birthday too."

He stood back up and spoke to Ed.

"Here, let me have your coats. You go ahead to the living room, you know the way."

As he hung up the coats the knocker sounded again. This was the first time I had heard so many people come to the front door in such rapid succession.

This time it was the Mortensen's from next door. They had closed the store and had their dinner before coming. Seven o'clock seemed to be the perfect time. Just as my chime sounded, the Mortensens, with Julius, came down the hall to join the rest of the group. There were fourteen, counting Mable Ann's friends. It was a small but pleasant gathering. Each family brought a gift for the birthday girl, and she was filled with excitement with the celebration, just for her.

"How are you tonight, Mr. Mortensen," Mable Ann inquired.

"Quite well, thank you, but I'd do a lot better if there was beer in my glass. How would it be if I trade you what I have behind my back for one?"

The other guest's expressions told the tale.
This was hardly something to say to a six-year old.
Unfortunately, I did recall other memories from the
last time he was at a party here.

"Not yet," Julius quickly interrupted. "I
have a gallon on the back porch, would that
satisfy you?"

Sam chided his friend. "A whole gallon,
you don't do that when I come over alone."

Julius responded in kind, "Well, if I did,
you'd drink too much?"

"Incidentally, how many of you would
like to have a glass of lemonade, since that is
what is in the gallon?"

Everyone smiled at the spontaneous joke
played on Morton and raised their hands, even
though the men might really have preferred beer.
They would have to go elsewhere to quench that
thirst. This was not their party; this was Mable
Ann's party.

Ed Nelson stood and held out his hand as he
introduced himself to Mr. Mortensen.

"I don't think we've met, my name is Ed
Nelson."

Morton took his hand and they shook.

"I am Hank Mortensen, Julius's neighbor,
and owner of the grocery store at the corner, but
everyone calls me Morton. This is my wife,
Edith."

Ed took his wife's hand and assisted her in
rising from the chair she was sitting in.

"And this is my wife, Priscilla." *Mr. Mortensen stood and took her hand. Sam and Kathleen were already know by everyone so their introductions were not necessary.*

After the introduction of little Letha Wadly and Mable Ann's other friends, everyone melded into groups, and the conversations started. I was quite interested in everything and listened intently. I was somewhat concerned that the young ladies had left the room, but soon I realized that they had quietly left the adults, and with Mable Ann they disappeared into the dining room, where a phonograph awaited them along with a new roll with the voice of Rudee Valley.

Priscilla, Ed's wife spoke, "I had a strange incident happen yesterday when I stepped out onto the back porch to get some things from the ice box. There was a savage standing there."

"A savage, do you mean an Indian?"

"Yes indeed, that is exactly what I mean! He frightened me."

"Did he threaten you?"

"No, he didn't do that. As a matter of fact I was pleasantly surprised that he was quite polite. I think he was hungry.

He pointed at the icebox where I had left some frozen meat to thaw in the sun. I gave him some of it and offered him a sandwich. He waited for me to fix it for him, and then he said something that I think meant 'thank you' and left as silently as he had arrived. It was then that I noticed the old gate to the alley had been repaired."

Molly looked at Catherine, "You see, that was the very thing that I was so concerned about. Aren't you worried?"

Catherine calmly looked at the women who had been listening, then made a sarcastic comment about the present situation, and then a memory from her childhood.

"Worried about the gate or the Indian?"

It was a sarcastic remark, but Catherine was tiring of people always being negative about these people.

She continued, "No mother, I am neither frightened nor worried. Do you recall when father told us about the time when he found the dead Indian boy at the river, and he felt that his company should take some responsibility. He told me that story many times and cried when he did.

"Yes, I remember that very well, but that was then, and this is now."

Catherine continued, "There are a lot of the plains people that are starving right here too. A small village is just over that hill," she pointed at the new Fairmont Park, "and they have very little of anything. I have also found they do little begging without returning the favor with some type of token, like repairing that broken gate."

Kathleen spoke up, "That's true. We are starting a group that hopes to take some food and clothing to them. They really need our help. After all, we did steal their land didn't we?"

There was no doubt that most of the older ladies found the story unsettling. Of course the younger ladies had not seen some of the bloodshed the older ones had, nor had they lived there during more trying times in Kaneville, the precursor of Council Bluffs.

Mr. Mortensen could not contain himself and interrupted their conversation, with his loud and discouraging commentary.

"When I first opened my store in the late 90's we had a lot of problems with those darn red-skinned thieves!"

"Isn't that a bit harsh?" Sam asked.

"Harsh? What do you mean harsh. You weren't here young man, but I was. Harsh is not even close to what I felt."

"Why? Did these people do something terrible to you?"

"Depends on how you look at it." His voice became louder. "Used to break into my store and steal me blind. Clothing, food, you name it, things they didn't have in the first place so I didn't figure they should be gettin' them from me?"

Sam persisted, "Maybe they were hungry and didn't know how else to get what they needed."

"Hogwash! There was game out there aplenty; rabbits, deer, pheasants, squirrels, fish, plenty for them to eat. There was work they could have done but no, they just stole enough corn from everyone hereabouts to make a meal and plant a field too!"

I could see that Mr. Mortensen was worked up. During his tirade he not only gobbled his glass of lemonade, but he gestured for a second one and almost drank it in one gulp as well. The other men tried to overlook his bad manners, but it was a difficult thing to do. I have set on the mantle of many parties and never been witness to such nonsense. Even the drunk at the restaurant that almost knocked down the Christmas tree back in Connecticut was not as belligerent as this man was becoming.

Julius spoke discretely, "Hank, perhaps you should settle down. After all it is the lady's conversation, isn't it?"

Then I saw something that I had never seen before, and hoped to see never again. Morton started smiling, stood, and picked up a glass ashtray.

"I bet none of you ever saw anything like this before."

Before anyone could say a word, or stop him, he pushed one of Catherine's crystal ashtrays into his mouth, and chewed it like it was a piece of hard candy. The glass crunched up as the guests gasped in disbelief. Never had they seen anything like that before. His poor wife stood and attempted to grab his hand, but he pulled it away from her.

"Leave me alone woman! I'll do what I damn well please, if you don't mind!"

Edith pleaded, "Please Hank, come with me. You don't want to ruin the child's party, do you?"

"Ruin the party! I am 'making' the party."

Then he winked at Catherine and asked his audience quite loudly if everyone saw what he did. Then he laughed.

"I didn't think so. I am the toughest man in Dane town."

He looked at each man, carefully examining them. Then he said again that he knew he was the toughest man there, and then he insanely challenged the rest to prove otherwise. I could not believe what I had just seen, and I felt certain there was no one there, other than his poor wife, who had been subjected to such behavior.

Half-pulling and half-steering Morton away, Edith attempted an apology.

"I think it is time for Hank and I to leave. He does work long hours, and sometimes a drink or two causes him to..."

Morton interrupted, "You don't need apologize for me. These people like me and they know what lemonade can do."

He pulled a flask from inside his coat pocket and winked at Julius, hoping for his neighbor to come to his aid. Instead, Julius in a gentlemanly manner, carefully took Hank's arm.

"Come now Hank, it's time for you to go home."

Begrudgingly he followed Edith to the front door while breaking loose from Julius's grip. Julius remained close behind to retrieve their coats for them.

Trying to continue being a gracious host, he told them, "I hope you enjoyed your evening, and thank you so much for Mable Ann's gift. We do hope to see you again."

I did not hear any other words, only the closing of the door. The party returned to normal and continued for some time. Mable Ann returned to the living room and opened her gifts; the children played a few games, with their parent's assistance. Soon the cake and ice cream was served, gentle conversation continued without further reference to either the Indians, who came from time to time asking for a handout, or Mr. Mortensen and his strange behavior. My gong struck nine, and it was as though all the lights in the world were about to be extinguished. The guests filed out of the living room in tandem, and gathered their children and coats.

The evening came to an end and Catherine took her aunt's hand.

"Thank you for coming. We're so glad you're living here now and can be with us. I just wish father could have..."

Molly interrupted, "So do we, sweetheart, and Jim too. Being close to you is such a blessing for us."

Then she looked at Catherine, "I am glad that Mable Ann knows that adults don't act like Mr. Mortensen." She cast her eyes toward the little one, "You do know that don't you Mable Ann?"

"Yes Grandma. Momma has told me that Mr. Mortensen gets sick sometimes."

Molly and Claudia left. Julius and Catherine tucked their beautiful little six-year old into bed, turned off the lights, and then retired to the sanctity of their boudoir after.

CHAPTER 25

1912 was the beginning of not only a new year, but a new era of progress in the United States. New Mexico became the 47th state in the union, Arizona the 48th and it was another presidential election year.

April 14th was a terrible day, when the huge passenger vessel, called the Titanic, sunk after hitting an iceberg in the Atlantic.

The new president, named Woodrow Wilson came into office, after beating out his rivals, a fellow named Teddy Roosevelt who represented his own new party called the Progressive Party, but nicknamed the Bull Moose Party, a second one named Howard Taft of the Republican party, and a third, Eugene Debs, of the Socialist Party? "What a field of opposition," as Don would have announced.(21)

It was early February when Sam and Kathleen stopped by. Kathleen needed some advice on marriage, and Sam for his weekly visit.

Sam sat on the couch across from Julius's chair and seemed to be deep in thought for a second or two, and then he asked,

"Are you still driving that Maxwell that your father-in-law left behind?"

"Yes, occasionally I am, why do you ask?"

"Well, Kathleen and I are planning a honeymoon, after the wedding of course, and I was considering buying a car, you know... a used one."

"And," Julius asked.

"Would you consider selling it to me?"

"I really haven't thought about selling it, it is barely a year old."

Sam forged ahead, "Well, since you have a truck now, and Catherine doesn't drive, I thought you might consider selling the car."

Julius seemed somewhat lost in thought. "I have not even thought about it. I'd have to talk to Catherine and Molly you know, it really is their car and I just drive it, since neither of them do."

"Would you talk to them and give it some thought, and let me know what they think."

Their brief chat was interrupted when Catherine and Kathleen entered the room.

"Guess what?" Catherine asked Julius.

"I have no idea. What?"

"Kathleen and Sam are going to take a a honeymoon after their wedding, isn't that wonderful?"

Julius tried to act surprised. "That sure is swell. Sam just told me about it,"

Catherine asked Julius, "Didn't I tell you that this visit was for something?"

"Yes you did Catherine and as usual, you were correct."

As he did from time to time, Julius stared off into space for what seemed an eternity, then he asked her a question.

"Why don't we sell your father's old car to them so they can go in style?"

"I don't know. How do you think daddy would feel?"

"I must admit I have no idea, but knowing how he thought, he'd probably say it was a fine idea." He stopped for a second then continued, "Of course if you feel we shouldn't ..."

"I don't know how I feel. I'll have to talk to mother, because I would need to know what she thinks before saying any more."

Sam and Kathleen acted uncomfortable. Sam stuck his finger under his collar, as though it was too tight. Kathleen looked down at the floor and moved her skirt back and forth in a nervous motion. She had no idea that he was going to ask to buy their car.

He took Kathleen's hand, and they stood, for what seemed like forever, looking questioningly at their friends.

Sam suggested to Kathleen that he thought they should be going.

The next morning, Catherine talked to her mother at some length. When she returned to her kitchen, she found Julius sitting at the table.

He spoke first. "I owe you an apology for yesterday."

"You do?"

"Yes, I do. Sam had already asked me if I would be willing to sell the car before you and Kathleen came into the room."

"And what did you tell him?"

"I told him I would have to talk to you and Molly before I could answer him."

"In other words, you knew all about that before you suggested it to me?"

"Yes, I did, and I shouldn't have put everyone ill at ease. Sam caught me off guard with his request, but when I thought about it, I felt it might be a nice thing for us to do. To tell the truth, I have been thinking about that new Chevrolet Company for some time. "

Catherine quickly picked up on the Chevrolet business.

"Oh, so that's what this is all about is it, a new car?"

She took a sip of some cold coffee that was in her cup. It took a minute or so to digest what Julius said, and to reconsider how she had answered.

"Mother thinks it is a good idea too, but she did have some concerns about how you might jam the five of us into your truck."

Julius mustered a small smile, "Do you both really think I would let our family be without a car?"

Catherine answered, "No, not really. Why don't you call Sam... but don't mention the new car idea."

"I won't, but I'm not done with that stinker yet. He has one coming."

"Now, if you are going to start teasing Sam by saying something about the new car, perhaps I should just call Kathleen."

"Oh, all right. I won't tease him, I swear."

The family was in agreement and now the deal had to be struck. This was my first time being close enough to hear the financial arrangements. Being able to hear from the very beginning, the deal being offered, and being accepted, was exciting for me.

Julius came into the hall and turned the crank on the telephone. The operator answered and asked him what number.

"The number is 23, operator."

There was a moment of waiting for the phone to be answered.

"Sam, this is Julius, about our discussion yesterday, what is your offer?"

I couldn't hear the voice on the other end. I knew by the pause that Sam was saying something.

"I think Six Hundred dollars might be a bit low, would you consider Six Hundred and Fifty dollars?"

There was a longer hesitation this time before Julius spoke again.

"You think that is a bit high? It is hardly a year old, and Don paid over Eight Hundred Dollars to get it here?"

Again, there was silence for several seconds while Sam was giving an answer. Suddenly, his voice became quite loud and I heard him plainly.

"Okay, I'll give you the Six Hundred and fifty dollars, but you do realize that the local dealer has gone out of business, and I will have to drive into Omaha to get everything done?"

Julius seemed to give some thought to his answer before answering.

"Okay, Six hundred then. A deal?"

Again, the silence was deafening, then the sound came through plainly.

"It's a deal. I can't wait to tell Kathleen."

Then silence, as Julius hung the receiver back on the box, and walked into the kitchen.

"Hon, we sold it. The car is gone."

"They will be happy, won't they?

There were a few seconds of silence, and Catherine asked a question, one that Julius knew would be coming after the deal was done.

"How soon can we go look at that new auto-car; the Chevrolet was it?" (22)

CHAPTER 26

January 7, 1912 arrived, Mable Ann's seventh birthday. This time, the party would be for her and her friends, more than just a family celebration. At least that was the way it was planned when I overheard the ladies talking.

It was exciting for me to see the preparations being made for the gala event. Molly and Aunt Claudia arrived a bit early, as they frequently did. Julius was home too, since it was a Sunday. Church had been skipped, because the preparations had to be made for food and drink. After all it was not everyday that someone turned seven years of age.

Mable Ann was dressed in her best clothes. Long black stockings and neatly snapped black shoes to match. Her red velvet dress was trimmed with lace at the end of the sleeves and around the hem that fell four inches below her knees. The red velvet belt with the large bow in the back matched perfectly. Of course the ribbon in her hair was a slightly different shade of red but edged in white lace as well.

It was always a great joy to see her friends come to the party. She had only a few, but they were quite special to her.

Margaret was a thin girl with a larger than life smile that radiated so that it lit the room. Unfortunately, she was not a healthy girl and her parents, Elsie and Charlie Johnson, guarded her closely as she could not play in all of the games. Her eyes were somewhat sunken and were a bit dull as they set so perfectly below her beautifully coiffured hair. Her dress was a plain grey one with sewed-on flower petals. Its long sleeves with lace at each wrist were quite stylish.

Elizabeth, the Mortensen's youngest, while not as pretty as Mable Ann she was still a very attractive little girl in her own way. Her dimpled cheeks gave way to a small and slightly uplifted nose, the top of which were met by thin red eyebrows. Her hair gave life to them with its soft shade of red. There were freckles, but they were of a very light nature.

Jenny, a school chum, was much like her name. Her shorter brown hair fell just below her petite shoulders. It was gathered with a blue striped ribbon tied close to her head which left the rest of it almost in a pigtail, but not woven, as they generally are. She had lovely brown eyes, a delightful face, that even when it was not smiling brought joy to your heart. Her dress was of a taffeta material and seemed to be almost stiff in nature and yet it moved gracefully with each step she took, much as a dress might cling slightly to a dancer. Like all the girls her age, it came below the knee and was met by her off-white long stockings that gave way to the black tie-up shoes.

The Fire chief's daughter, Joan was dressed equally well. She wore an exquisitely styled burgundy colored velvet dress with a deep red bow on the back. The color favored her well and the long stockings matched the black buckled shoes that she wore. Her long black hair hung well below her neckline. She had enchanting blue eyes that gleamed like jewel stones from each side of her petite little nose.

Mable Ann's favorite friend, Letha Wadly, was a homely little girl that Mable Ann loved so much. She was Mable Ann's favorite school chum and confidant, and one who seemed to be a lasting forever type. Her clothing did not seem as elegant, yet she stood out among the others for a reason I cannot explain. Perhaps it was the breeding that emanated with every word she spoke. Every word was perfect, as were her manners. While her beauty may not have been as visible as the other young ladies, her enchantment remained unexplainable.

As girls do, they giggled and laughed at every little thing. Julius teased them until he felt he should stop, and he retreated into the parlor to sit in his big chair.

Mother and Grandmother busied themselves with serving refreshments and overseeing the children as they played.

There were a few parlor games from the old parlor game book that came from Catherine's youth. Its rules were studied before eating.

The long anticipated deserts of the afternoon were spotlighted by the special birthday cake that was adorned with seven lit candles.

Watching them, as Mable Ann made her wish and blew the candles, brought brought back memories of when Catherine was that age, and her childhood parties, back in Waterbury so long ago.

After the celebration was over, and the guests had left, Catherine brought in a large box and gave it to Mable Ann.

Excitedly, Mable Ann asked, "Oh Mother, what is it? It is so big. She shook it gently, and listened, but could hear nothing, "May I open it now?"

Catherine smiled, "Of course you may. If you didn't want to, I would be surprised!"

Ever so carefully, as if she were afraid it would break, Mable Ann removed the ribbon and bow, watchfully laying them beside her on the floor. Next, she slid her finger into the open area of the wrapping, where it overlapped itself, and ran it down the opening, being careful not to cut her finger on the paper. The paper readily fell open, and a plain cardboard box appeared before her widening eyes. She removed the lid, and there, staring back at her, was a beautiful doll, lying on pink silk material that had been left over, no doubt, from a dress made long before.

"Oh, she is beautiful. I don't know what to say. Her face is so pretty. I think I will call her Katrina, from the book you read to me called the "Silver Skates." Would that be a good name?"

Catherine looked at her and answered,

"I think that would be a wonderful name for her."

Mable Ann removed the doll from the box, and held her lovingly in front of her. The doll was half as tall as she was. It had delicate porcelain hands; its feet tucked into little leather shoes, just like her's. The dress was a taffeta material, and the underskirts were of linen, very similar to the ones that she wore.

"Mother look, is this coat just like yours? "After closer examination she was positive, "It is exactly like yours! Did you make it?"

Catherine looked at her with love. "No, I didn't honey, your Grandmother Holscomb made the coat, and your Grandmother Jepsen made the dress and underskirt. Aren't they lovely?"

As they were admiring the doll, the door opened and Julius stepped into the room. "Look at what I found in the workshop little one."

Mable Ann turned to look and she saw a beautiful wooden cradle. There was no doubt that her father had made it for the doll. It was his part of his little one's birthday gift. It fit the doll perfectly. It had a slatted bottom and slatted sides. Each of the four corners was made of a slightly ornate post. The rounded wooden platforms on the bottom allowed it to rock so that Mable Ann could put her new doll to sleep whenever she felt it was naptime. She rushed to her father, and he gathered her up in his arms.

"Oh daddy, this is so wonderful. Thank you so much."

He looked down at her smiling face and told her whom else she must thank.

"You also have to thank your Aunt Claudia, because she painted it for you."

The 1912 Indianapolis 500 came on the 30th of January, and was won by Joe Dawson, driving a Marmon car. (another strange name)

Later, on October the 16th the World Series was won by the Boston Red Socks when they defeated the New York Giants. (I have to tell you I can't understand how a pair of socks, of any color, could defeat a giant, whether they were from Boston, New York, or anywhere else!)

CHAPTER 27

It was already 1913 and *early one day in February, the doorknocker sounded. Julius was standing by the door and he opened it find that his friend was waiting to be let in.*

"Come on in Sam, I haven't seen you since Mable Ann's birthday. Where have you been?"

Julius's inquisitiveness about the whereabouts of his friend was obvious. He had not come around for his weekly visits, and this was a first.

"I have been here and there. We have been so busy at the office; putting in many hours and then going home to rest."

Julius voiced his concern, "We haven't seen you for so long that we were concerned that maybe… well maybe there was a problem with…"

"No problem. Kathleen and I plan to get married and take that honeymoon I have promised her. I finally asked her father's permission, and he surprised me when he gave it to me."

"Really, and he did so without provisions?"

Julius poured some coffee for his friend.

"Well, yes there were some."

"Like?" Julius questioned.

"He insists the children be raised Catholic, and he would like me to change my faith as well."

"And?"

"I told him that we would raise the children as Catholic, as he wished, but that I would not change my religious beliefs. I had been a Methodist too long for that."

"And he agreed?"

"It has been a yearlong fight, but finally, he gave in. You know I have been, or I should say, Kathleen and I, have been, working on him for over a year. I think my promotion at work helped the situation however, and having a car didn't hurt either."

"Those things always seem to have value don't they? I don't know how I would react, should Mable Ann decide to marry outside her mother's faith."

Julius took a sip of his coffee before he continued. It was a day long in coming, and there were considerations to be made, but there was little concern that their love would be able to overcome them.

"I think it would be a difficult decision to make."

"I am sure that is true. It is both Kathleen's and my decision however, that the children should decide, when they are old enough to do so, the religion they truly believe is right for them."

Sam just stopped by to deliver the good news. He was on a tight schedule, as he indicated to Julius, and had to leave much sooner than he would have liked to. The year seemed to boom along as though it were a shot from cannon, especially since the wedding was planned for May 1st,

The date was just around the corner when Kathleen stopped to see Catherine with a request.

"Catherine, would you be my Matron of Honor?

Catherine was beside herself with joy. "I would love to do that. I have been waiting in the hope you would ask me. Yes, yes, yes."

"There is another thing too. Would you allow Mable Ann to be my flower girl? My nephew, who is going to be eight this year, will be the ring bearer."

"Absolutely, what a cute couple they will make since they are almost the same height."

May quickly arrived. Kathleen had been at the house several times to speak with not only Catherine, but Molly, Anna, and Claudia as well. She felt their input was absolutely necessary, even though most of the input was done by her mother. The preparations were many and the planning had taken several months to complete. It seemed the door was opened and closed so many times the hinges could have fallen off. The flowers, the reception hall, the church, the dresses...I am so glad I am just a clock, I don't think being a human would be good for me.

As I listened to all of the preparations being made, I discovered that this being a Catholic Wedding, there were even more preparations necessary than for the Presbyterian one that I had witnessed in Connecticut. There are the special classes for Sam that gives him the true meaning of confirmation and communion. They suggested he should be baptized once again, but he refused to go that far. It was also discovered that since he was not a Catholic, they would be restricted from standing behind the communion rail for their blessing. There were a few other things that I deemed unimportant, since I am not the one getting married and have no religion to understand.

The days finally came and I heard that the wedding went off without a problem. Mable Ann was, of course, a beautiful flower girl in her pink satin dress, that was decorated with small white lace petals.

I was pleased that I could see her as she preened in front of the mirror across from my fireplace home.

Molly and Claudia found a veil and attached it to the crowning headpiece that they said made her face "glow like an angel."

I was not privy to see the bride and groom, nor did I see the ring bearer, but from what I overheard it was a beautiful wedding. I understand that the couple disappeared immediately after the reception, in a Maxwell car, for points unknown.

The year continued on with birthdays and holidays, but it seemed that one of the newest big events of the year is baseball which is definitely growing into a national past time.

On October the 16th the World Series was won by the Boston Red Socks when they defeated the New York Giants.

(I have to confess that I still can't understand how a pair of socks of any color, could defeat a giant whether they were from Boston, New York or anywhere else! I also was wondering if the New York Giants were related some way to Jack Johnson since he was also a giant.)

CHAPTER 28

1914 came quickly. Sam returned to his old habit of weekly visits, and on one such occasion, Julius decided some discussions needed to take place about politics. While trying not to attack his friend, Julius did seem to come on rather strongly.

"What do think of this new tax law that they have added up there in Washington?"

Sam answered, "I assume you are talking about another amendment that is to become a tax law? I have been so out of touch with anything but work lately that I have paid very little attention to what has been happening."

Julius's expression became stern, and he could not believe that his friend had not heard about this new amendment.

"They have been talking about it for some time now, for at least a year. There are those that were able to keep it from happening, up until recently. Now, as you know, we have this new Wilson fellow, as our sitting president. He and his party have the power."

Sam took a quick sip of his tea, then, with a concerned look, he spoke to his friend. "I have been out of touch. What does it all mean?"

Julius leaned forward in his chair, and rested his chin on his hands and his elbows on his knees. In a low voice, almost a whisper, he acted as though he was about to divulge a secret.

"As I understand it, this Amendment Sixteen, as they call it, was ratified by congress on February 3rd. It seems to indicate, that starting now, we will have to pay a tax on any money we earn, regardless where, or how, we make it." (23)

Sam sat erect, "Is that legal? I thought our parents and grandparents came here to avoid tax without representation."

"That's the way it has been for the most part, but you know this is not the first time the government has done this."

"Not the first time?"

"Nope, not the first time, after the last war we had a tax to offset the cost of it. Of course that war is over, but it appears we have overspent again, or at least the government has, and now to catch up, they need to collect this new tax."

Sam took another sip of his tea before he asked his next question.

"Then this is a temporary thing, just until the government catches up with its spending?"·

"Sam, you know as well as I do that once it starts, it will never stop. I guess we can be thankful it isn't that much."

"You say, that much? It seems to me that anything they take from us it too much! Don't you agree?"

"Yes, I do agree."

"Tell me, how much?"

Julius sat back in his chair, and took a deep breath, as he considered his answer.

"Don't quote me on this, because it is vaguely written, but as I understand it, we first have to make more than $3000.00 a year. At that time we will be able to deduct a set amount for us and our families, around $2500.00 I believe. Then we can deduct all the interest we pay out, and any business losses.

For instance, farmers can deduct costs caused by storms and such. I am not sure about any tax break for you or me. Those with deductions will have to pay 1% on the balance."

"Well that's a relief. Maybe they will tire of the bookwork, and drop the whole thing when they see how little they receive."

"We can only hope," Julius repeated softly, "we can only hope."

Both men settled into their chairs and seemed to be in their own world for a bit before either of them spoke.

Julius broke the silence, "So tell me, how do your folks feel about the compromise you had to make?"

"What compromise?"

"Good gracious man, the compromise in your religion of course."

"Oh, that one, well, needless to say, they were not delighted at all. As a matter of fact, my father got so red in the face I feared for his health."

"Did he get over it?"

"Yes, mother calmed him down quite nicely, but I think he was still upset. I am praying that by the time June rolls around, both sets of parents can come to an understanding, for the kids' sakes, you know."

Julius sat up straight in his chair, "For the kid's sake?"

Sam answered in a calm voice, "Yes, and ours as well."

"Wait now, you said kids! What are you talking about? You have no children.

Sam had certainly aroused the curiosity of his friend with that small word, "kids." Could this be a hint as to the future, and perhaps the growth of the family at Sam's place? My curiosity was aroused, and I wondered why I had not overheard Molly and Kathleen speaking of this event.

Sam raised himself up from his chair using its arms to lean on.

"Yes, I am getting older suddenly, and will soon be the father of twins!"

"Twins? How has Kathleen been able to conceal such a thing. She is still small and petite, not round bellied as one would expect. You have to be joking!"

Sam smiled, knowing he had pulled off a good one on his friend by withholding the information that Kathleen was with child, as a matter of fact, two of them.

"Julius, you are soon to become godfather for twins, isn't that wonderful?"

There was no doubt that Julius had been shocked. He was speechless, and when he recovered from the shock of it all and regained his mental being, his chest seemed to swell with pride. Of course it didn't really swell up, so to speak, but I have heard the expression before and thought it fitting at this time.

As it turned out, Molly was equally taken by surprise about the wonderful new thing that was taking place. Kathleen had kept the pregnancy very secret, as Sam had always said that a family should keep things private, but now her small frame had grown, although hidden by the hoop skirts everyone saw her wearing. Now I knew why there was no gossip for me to hear.

The twins finally arrived on June 2, Don's birthday. The agreement regarding the matter of faith had settled down and the bickering was over. Of course the children would be raised in the Catholic faith, as agreed, but time would be the teller of all, when the twins were old enough to have a say in their own lives.

The year continued with history in the making. The Grand Central Station was rebuilt into the largest depot in the world.

The Panama Canal finally opened when the president pushed the button and blew up the Gambo Dike that held the water back.

Medical practices were improving with the second non-direct blood transfusion was performed by Albert Hustin of Belgium. (24).

One hot afternoon in August, Sam stopped by the house to see Julius, who had been working feverously in his shop for several hours. The door was open, as was the window in the parlor, and the outside conversations wafted through the house like the air upon which they floated.

"Good afternoon Julius, you're sweating like a mule, what have you been working so hard on?"

"Sam, haven't you heard about the new government mandate, the one by Representative Sabath?" (25)

"No, I guess I haven't. What is it about?"

"Apparently Adolph Sabath, from Illinois, got an act passed that established a new department. Buildings close to the railroad depots will be rented to the government as a place for the immigrants coming into the country from the East to stay."

Sam sounded puzzled. "What kind of protection do they need?"

I could hear Julius wipe the accumulated sweat from his brow on the large red handkerchief he carried in his overall pocket.

"I don't suppose you have heard about the nativist movement either, have you?" (26)

"Nope, can't say that I have. What is it?"

"The way it was explained to me down at the court house last week, was that it means folks don't want any more immigrants coming in because they think they are too dumb or something, to be a part of our culture here."

Sam sounded agitated, "Now that's a bit disgusting don't you think? Where in the world would we be if everyone thought like that? Shucks, we are all immigrants aren't we?"

"I agree, but as I recall, not too long ago you were upset about the heavy-weight fight. Wasn't that Johnson fellow a refugee?"

Sam stammered, "That's different, these folks aren't of color."

Julius answered, knowing the message would be understood by Sam.

"Oh, really?"

Rather than continue the conversation that could escalate into an argument, Julius changed the subject back to the job he was working on.

"When they asked if I knew anyone who would be interested in helping on the project, I just said yes right away. It seemed to me to be a great way to make some money, as long as the government was going to pay for it. Maybe I'll get some of that tax money back I might be giving them."

Sam asked, "How is that going to help you in the carpentry business?"

Julius turned to look at his friend, then he answered.

"Well you see, they need these places, close by the depots, where folks can have some shelter, food, and a place to sleep without being molested, so-o-o-o," Julius drew out his word for emphasis as he put his thumb into his overall strap, "I am building bed frames, tables, and such, to fill the buildings they rent close by our depots. You know we have two of them, and one is right up the street."

"I have to say that you are enterprising Julius. Being down there at the court house is paying off for you, isn't it?"

"Yes, it sure is. And everyone thought I was a fool for lowering myself to being a janitor. Of course being an Alderman doesn't hurt either."

"I guess you fooled them, didn't you?"

Julius answered with a simple, "Yup, think so. Let's go inside where it is cooler."

Sam, not wanting his friend to have a 'one up' on him, asked him if he was aware of the new waterfowl law.

"Have you heard what those two East Republican senators did to us?"

"I don't know what you mean. What did 'who' do to us? Was it something personal?"

"No, nothing personal, unless you call telling us when we can, and when we can't, go hunting, personal."

Julius loved to hunt and fish. The time never was right to leave his work, but on the other hand, the time to work could be daunting, and a reprieve of sorts was needed from time to time. (Like every Sunday while Catherine was at church, when he could get away with it)

Julius answered excitedly, "Are you telling me that they are going to prohibit hunting?"

"Not exactly, but they are trying to stop us from hunting in the spring." (27)

Julius's face was turning that tell-tale color of red. It was that look that told anyone that knew him, his patience was being tried.

"Stopping us from spring hunting? I've never heard of such a thing! What kind of fools would do that? Who are these 'high and mighties' that want to do such a terrible thing?"

Sam made an attempt to settle Julius down a bit, "Now, don't let the blood rush to your head Julius, you know how you get."

"Who are they?"

"A couple of senators, I think they are from Massachusetts and Connecticut."

"Well I intend to write them a letter. I have a thing or two to say about that! Some of the best hunting is when those birds come back up from the South. I bet they never hunted a day in their lives!"

Sam did know something that Julius had not heard about, and the thorn in Julius's shoe really started tormenting his foot. I had not heard him as upset before, and I have to admit that while it was frightening to hear such a temper, it was also a bit humorous to know that someone could get the best of him.

Sam spoke quietly, "Now listen Julius, I don't think you should write them, at least not until you settle a bit. Let's have a cup of tea, for the nerves, first?"

"Of course you are right, no good ever came out of anger, but I get so danged mad when some do-gooder gets involved in something that is none of his business."

Winter was on its way and Thanksgiving had come and gone. Catherine's birthday arrived and departed, Christmas hustled through, and the New Year was on the horizon once again.

Sam and Kathleen, along with their twins, Sophia and Joan, stopped by to see their little God-daughter, Mable Ann, and to wish the Johnsons, Molly and Claudia, a great new year. It was, as always, good to see company come, and hopefully hear about new and exciting things that were going to take, or had already taken place. I wasn't disappointed on this visit.

"Come in, it's cold out there."

Sam remarked, "I hardly knocked on the door when you opened it. You must have been waiting for us to arrive."

Julius smiled, "No, as a matter of fact, I was just hanging my hat on the hook.

Julius took their hats and coats and placed them into the hall closet, and then he escorted them into the parlor.

"It's good to see you," Catherine said as she entered the room, "it's been a while since Thanksgiving, how have you two been?"

Kathleen, for a change seemed chatty. "We have been busy. It seems that ever since the twins arrived we have been too busy to go anywhere. We were glad that you stopped by on your birthday, and then again on Thanksgiving morning before we went to my folks. We just can't seem to find time to go anywhere. When you stopped by we were so pleased to see someone, and just chat for a bit. When Christmas came we had to divide our time between both sets of parents. It seems we have no time to ourselves at all."

Sam chimed in, "Besides all of that, my work has doubled at the office. I have had two building designs to complete this past year."

Julius sat in his chair and listened to the chit-chat for a while, then he asked one of those debatable questions he seemed to come up with on a frequent basis.

"I guess you have heard that the Ford Company started off the year of 1914 by introducing an eight hour day and an extremely high wage of $5.00 per hour?" (29)
Sam answered him, "No, we haven't."

Sam looked at his wife and whispered carefully.

"He's hot again about something."

Julius ignored his friend's whispered comment.

"This has really made a lot of business owners mad, even me!

Do you realize that this kind of increase will cause problems with the profits of any company and even force layoffs to occur?"

"Julius, it doesn't do any good to get upset! People are always going to want more money, and with the unions in the minefields wanting to help more people! You know they aren't going to stay out of this company fray for long.

Besides, after having the twins, I understand more than before about how costs are going up and we all need more money."

Julius intervened, "I suppose, but that doesn't mean I have to like it. Why can't we just stay like we are, and let things happen on their own?"

Sam could not control his feelings and raved, "Because, if things stayed the same you wouldn't have that new Chevrolet car, I wouldn't be designing new buildings, and our wives would not have any modern appliances, that's why!"

I could see things were not going well and both wives were fidgeting. Kathleen wisely made a suggestion.

"Well, we just wanted to stop by and wish you folks a happy New Year, right dear?"

She gave Sam what you could call an evil eye. He realized he had almost boiled over.

"Yes, of course hon, you're right, we have to get over to your folks place."

Catherine asked, "You're not leaving already are you?"

Kathleen answered, "Yes, I'm afraid so. We just wanted to stop by for a few minutes. When are you coming to visit us again?"

Julius, without answering Kathleen's question, asked them, "How about a cup of tea before you leave?"

Catherine gave Julius an unpleasant look as she answered for them both.

"We will, soon. Right now we are having a time problem with the new cabinets, and the other things Julius has been working on. Then, of course, there are those normal problems with children. I don't envy your having two of them."

Sam and Kathleen stood and Sam gave a polite kiss to Catherine's cheek, shook Julius's hand, and asked them both to tell their God-daughter "Happy New Year" for them.

I was sure that Julius didn't catch the expressions on the faces of their friends as I did, but it was easy to see my thoughts were correct, that they were not in the mood for more of Julius's raving, right or wrong.

On the following Saturday, Charlie and Elsie came to visit. It had been some time since they had stopped by, so while the visit was unexpected, it was an appreciated one. Charlie, as usual, stayed on the front porch, even though it was a bit chilly, to just sit in the sun and enjoy his pipe. Julius stayed with Charlie, while Elsie went into the kitchen to spend some time with Catherine. I was fortunate enough to hear the conversation, through the partially opened parlor window, as Charlie and Julius talked.

Julius asked, "How are things at the nursery?"

Charlie removed the pipe from his mouth and after some contemplation, he slowly answered.

"Good as can be spected I suppose, not much happening."

Julius stated, "Not much going on huh? I sometimes wish I could say that, I have been so busy. There's a lot of carpentry work going on."

"Really, I haven't paid no attention."

With the Ford company still on his mind, Julius was bound to get involved with some conversation about the wages and weekly hours.

"What do you think about Henry Ford and his new work principles, up there in Detroit, Michigan?"

Charlie blew some smoke from his mouth, and appeared to think about the question before answering.

"Haven't heard nothin' about it."

It had momentarily slipped Julius's mind about the illiteracy of his friend.

"It's been in the newspaper quite a lot, as of late."

Charlie took a couple of drags on his pipe, tapped the bowl against the porch railing, and stuck it into his coat pocket.

"I don't read English you know. I leave all of that up to Elsie. If she sees something she thinks I ought to know about, she tells me."

Julius answered, "I forgot about that."

Charlie, noticed his friend's uneasiness, and changed the subject.

"Most folks don't pay no attention. I think it's nice the way you folks do, though."

"Pay attention to what?"

"Attention to us, that's what."

"That's just what friends do."

Charlie again weighed his answer before he spoke.

"Julius, what did you say old Henry was doin' up north?"

"He is giving five dollars an hour to those auto workers, and giving them eight hour days too."

"Must be nice, I'm still gittin' the usual."

"And what is that?"

Charlie looked out at the yard, and nonchalantly answered, "Two-fifty a day and still workin' ten hours or so every day, 'ceptin' Sunday, of course."

Julius told him that, he thought maybe Henry was trying to stay ahead of the unions and that the new mechanized production lines probably were a part of the new wage and the less hour thing too.

Charlie grunted his answer, "Pro'bly so."

I understood that Charlie was not much on conversation and it was assumed that since he didn't read, he didn't keep up with the times. Now, I can't read either, but having all of Julius's friends come by with their news of the day is certainly in my favor and with that talking box, I do keep pretty well informed.

Julius continued, "As I understand it, the mine workers might come up with something new, since they are working with a union of their own."

"Really?"

Charlie seemed surprised and pulled the pipe out of his pocket, and reloaded the bowl from his tobacco pouch.

"Yes, in fact, they are asking for shorter hours, and at least two-dollars and fifty cents a day. That's still a long ways from what Ford is paying."

"Maybe I oughta look into another line of work."

Charlie took a drag from his pipe and blew some smoke into the air.

"But then again, that would mean I'd have to learn to read and write English, and I don't want to do that. Too much effort, and I'm gettin' along pretty good with Elsie doin' the English part, while I just keep my readin' and writin' in Danish, from and to my friends back home.

"Probably so," Julius reluctantly agreed.

I remember, from earlier conversations that I have overheard in the kitchen between Julius and

Catherine, about how nice it would be if Charlie had more initiative and would learn English. (I don't understand what that really means, English, Danish or whatever.)

There are days that I am thankful, that all I have to do is tick-tock, and I even leave that up to the works. Maybe I am like old Charlie, and don't even know it?

Charlie and Elsie left after a delightful afternoon and Julius switched on that talking box.

It told us that a group of National Guard men attacked some striking coal miners in a place called Ludlow, and they killed twenty-four of them. There seemed to be a lot of news coming from it than from Julius and Catherine's visitors

Time continued to move forward, and soon it was thea 14th of May. Julius came down the stairs and went directly into the parlor where Catherine was considering breakfast preparation.

"Good morning sweetheart."

Catherine stopped momentarily and asked, "And why are you so chipper today?"

Julius answered, "It's a special day, that's why?"

Without changing her expression, or slowing down in her moving toward the kitchen, she asked him a question.

"What day would that be?" Julius wrapped his arms around her waist from behind, and pulled her closely to him, as he gently whispered into her ear.

"Happy Mother's Day."

This year it fell on Sunday, and church was scheduled. Julius agreed to go, in light of the day, even though he thought of many other things he would rather do. He still appeared to feel his agnostic belief was the proper one, regardless of whatever others might believe. At most a deviation from what I thought he was going to do after a previous conversation I overheard, when he told her "and our heaven...now."

"Well Mr. Johnson, you had best sit down to your breakfast. Remember you are going with the rest of us to the services today."

"I haven't forgotten hon, I know what I agreed to. Besides, it's Mother's Day, the second one on our soil, and I want to see all of the fancies at church today."

"That is not a proper reason to attend the services, and you know that."

Catherine's voice indicated her disapproval of his comment. She was not pleased and he knew it; God's day was now initiated for evermore at the Julius Johnson household and Julius had best not forget it.

Mable Ann, who had been taking it all in, with a sudden brightness in her voice, asked her father a question.

"Won't it be nice for you to be with us at church today daddy?"

"Yes it will little one, I am looking forward to going with you very much."

"Okay, both of you, if you don't start eating we will be late."

It is refreshing to hear them bicker and make comments, and in a good and happy way. Life seemed to be pretty good for most folk, but as the year wore on, things started to change.

That wooden box that sat in the corner of the living room told about men fighting in places I had never heard of before, Germany and Russia, Turkey and France, and Hungary and Austria. I wondered where are these places? Are they near Nebraska, or back by Massachusetts and Connecticut? They certainly must be places far away from where we are.

I am so glad to be a clock, and being where I am but every time that box talks, it seems to talk about war. It affects so many people that I think it must be a contagious thing, like the small pox that I heard about during some of Don's conversations.

I was glad when fall came. Thanksgiving was here, and the festivities would be beginning from now through Christmas. The special tablecloth was retrieved from its resting place in the buffet drawer, along with the matching napkins with their pumpkins and corn stock decoration on them. I wished I could smell things, because everyone always remarks how the smell that the cooked and baked specialties of the ladies, is so fragrant and makes the house so special.

Christmas Julius took Catherine and Mable Ann to the woods outside of town. They brought back a big tree for Christmas that was much like the one at the old place in Waterbury. It stood tall, clear up to the ceiling.

It would soon be decorated with those pretty strings of popcorn, the little soldiers painted red and blue, and of course the many carved out figures from Julius's workshop. Christmas carols would be sung and people would laugh and seem to be nicer to each other than any other time of the year. Even those Brits and the Germans, who seem to fight all the time, would stop fighting on Christmas day.

Catherine received a new dress and hat, Julius got another gadget or two for his shop, and of course, Mable Ann was the big winner with the presents that arrived from all of the relatives, just for her.

It took the edge off of the unhappy things that seemed to be happening according to that talking box. The year was coming to a close and I think, that under the circumstances, it is a good thing.

The parties continue, although it seems to me, less happy than before, but still wonderful.

Mable Ann and her friends spread games out on the floor and stayed inside where I could see them play. Many fourth ward constituents of Julius's came to visit, and I could hear and see them, and learn of the city problems and achievements. It reminded me of the old days in Waterbury, at the restaurant, when the travelers, and people from the stores, would all come in and enjoy the foods, and the fragrances that enhanced them.

I was fascinated to see how each candleholder was placed so carefully, so that when they were lit, they couldn't ignite a branch and burn the tree, or worse, set fire to the house where I would be burned like kindling.

Of those things that I could not understand, one was why the people didn't stop fighting. What happened to the "Good will toward men" they keep singing about? I will never understand why people can't be like us clocks. We never fight, we just tell folks the time and tend to our own business.

CHAPTER 29

1915 came, and I had hoped for be a better year than 1914. Unfortunately I was disappointed. It started out badly as the talking box told us about some kind of an infection that folks caught from a hospital. It was something they didn't want, but was given to them anyway, by someone called Mary. I think it was called Typhoid Fever.

Then there were those foolish folks fighting again, the Germans who poisoned some Russian people, another bunch of strangely named folks, the Ottoman Turks that killed several Armenians.

Maybe it's those strange names, or maybe something in the water? I know I am glad to be here, on this mantle, where I am safe instead of those places that seem to have so much turmoil. It seems to me that they must act like Mable Ann does, when her mother says, "She acts that way because she is just a child."

In May, that wonderful day that has always been filled with love around the places I have spent my time that they call Mother's Day, arrived. While there was no peace in the world, there was love around the Johnson and Holscomb homes.

"Good morning, and do you know what today is?"

"Of course I do. It is Mother's Day."

Julius told Caatherine, "I have something special for you today."

Catherine asked, "Flowers, my favorites?"

"Nope, not this year, this year it is something very special and I hope that you like it."

I heard Julius as he stepped out of the kitchen door and onto the back porch. He retrieved whatever it was that he had been working on, and brought it into the kitchen. I could hear the joy in Catherine's voice when Julius presented her with his gift.

"Oh Julius, it is beautiful, when did you ever have time to do this?"

He only told her what was necessary, not wanting to let her know how many hours he had spent making the gift.

"A bit now, a bit then, actually I have been working on it for some time now; it was designed especially for you, because you are so special to me."

"I have always wanted a beautiful quilt rack."

"I know you have, and this one matches the headboard. Can you see that?"

He beamed with pride in his achievement and when he returned to the kitchen, Catherine answered his question.

"Yes I do, and it is beautiful."

I could hear the rustling of clothing, and the shuffle of feet, both indicating that a hug was taking place, no doubt in appreciation of this quilt rack thing he had made for her.

Julius carried it from the kitchen down the hall to the staircase, then he went up the stairs. I could hear him as he slid it carefully to set it in the center of the footboard of the bed.

Molly had wanted one like this too, but although Don tried to find one, he could not, at least could not find one that would match the bed boards like this one. It takes a carpenter like Julius to do the fine work required.

The year continued on and unfortunately, it was very little different from the year before. I was actually beginning to like the box that sat on the floor beside me in the parlor. It told me many things, for instance:

William Jennings Bryant resigned from his office as Secretary of State because he didn't agree with the president about something he said to the German people.

Some fellow named Babe Ruth hit a home run against another fellow named Jack Warhop. (Apparently this has some significant meaning to those that watch the new national past time baseball.) I can't get the gist of it at all. The "home run" thing, or running against someone, or another strange term, "Striking out." I felt that "Throwing a ball" sounded even stranger to me, what else would you do with a ball but throw it? It is another language to me.

Some human named Jimmy Lavender did something called "pitching." He belonged to a team called the "Chicago Cubs." This "pitching tribute" was called a "no hitter" and I think it was against another team called the New York Yankees. Now I have reached another part of that language that evades me. Why is it that anyone would be proud to be a cub, a baby bear?

I also have a difficult time figuring out why someone would have to identify themselves as a Yankee when they come from this country. No matter how long I am allowed to tick, I will never understand some of the silly things these humans say.

1916 came and things didn't change much. I did manage to pick up some interesting news from time to time.

A lady, by the name of Emma Goldman, got arrested over something about folks needing to stop having children. I didn't understand that either. I thought having children was something humans just did! (30)

There was a fellow named William Newton (31) who invented something that is used to turn on and turn off electric things. It was called a light switch. The idea being, that folks won't have to walk to the center of the room and turn off a light using that cord hanging down. It seems to me that the exercise would be good. There are many times that I have wished I could walk over and do that from time to time. It gets very tiresome, just sitting the way I have to.

The things these humans come up with to keep them from having to move around baffles me.

The other day Catherine received her Saturday Evening Post and was quite excited when she told Molly about a painting that was used on the cover. Some artist, named Norman Rockwell, painted it. In his painting, he depicted a "Boy and a Baby Carriage." I guess this kind of painting must be something special. I am sure that there isn't a clock around that could do it.

It seems to me that more women are doing things than they used to do, so maybe one of them will paint something.

Another lady named Margaret Sanger, got involved with that "stop having children" thing by opening a business that does something called birth control.

Jeanette Rankin was elected to the House of Representatives. I understand that was a wonderful achievement for the ladies.

It appears that each year more and more ladies are getting involved in things. That is probably good. I have noticed that they seem to have a way of quieting down the men-folks. I suppose the day will come when they will be handling just about everything.

Those strange named folks, the ones who want to fight all the time, have gone into the air to do it now. Those Wright brothers come to mind. They're the ones that build those gliders, those boxes with wings of sorts; they probably had something to do with it.

It appears that the German people are trying flying this time too. They are going to fly something called a Fokker against the Brits who fly their Sopwith Camel. Now here we go again, and I have to ask, what in the world is a camel doing, trying to fight with a piece of soap, in, or out, of the air?"

Time has passed so quickly that it's almost time for another New Year's Eve party. I am looking forward to it, since we haven't had nearly as many parties as we did in Connecticut.

It is my understanding that not only are the usual folks coming this year, but also that fellow I have heard so much about, General Dodge. They are saying that it will be an honor, if he does come, as he generally only gets involved with what they call 'high society'. Maybe it has something to do with Julius being one of those alder 'whatevers'.

"Have we made the list and sent the invitations yet?" Molly inquired.

"Yes mom, we have. I know I should have consulted you first, but I have invited your friends, as well as ours. I even invited General Dodge this time."

"Even General Dodge? Didn't you know he has passed away?"

"Are you sure, mom?"

"Yes I am quite sure, last January in fact." Molly was quite positive. (32)

Catherine could not believe what she had done.

"I feel badly now, since I already have mailed the invitation."

"I am sure that someone will respond dear, everyone makes mistakes."

Catherine looked relieved and smiled at her mother's comforting answer.

"I know mom, that they do, but why did I have to, and at this time?"

Nothing more was said (that I could hear anyway) and the day ended as quietly as it had begun. I felt let down, as I had been looking forward to listening to the General. He would, no doubt, have had some insight into this war thing that I was hearing so much about.

New Year's Eve arrived, and the family was waiting for the guests to arrive. Anna was already there, along with with Molly and Claudia. Mable Ann, now the grand old age of twelve, was allowed to stay up until ten o'clock on this special evening. It would be exciting for her to mingle with the older guests; and far past her normal eight o'clock bed curfew too!

The family waited impatiently for the for their guests. Finally the first of the guests arrived! The Sam Nelsons stepped onto the porch.

"Good to see you again Sam, you are the first to arrive, come on in..."

Sam responded, "We will, thank you, and thanks for the invitation. We were thrilled that my parents wanted to have the twins for the evening so we could come. We really needed a night with friends. The warmth of your fireplace will feel marvelous tonight, as there is a definite chill in the air."

Kathleen added, "Your home is always warm and friendly."

The evening continues with new guests coming, introductions being made, and greetings of the season being offered.

The group is not big, but the idea, as I understand from the conversations I heard during the planning, was not supposed to be too big, but rather intimate. The usual folks were there. Sam and Kathleen, Anna, Val and Mae, the Mortensens (and I hoped he didn't eat any more glass, or even worse, decide to try clocks for his dessert) Charlie and Elsie, and one new person, Miriam Huxley, the librarian,.

Julius first introduced Miriam to the group since this was her first time attending their party.

"Please everyone, I would like you to meet Miss Huxley, our new librarian."

Miss Huxley, typical of a librarian, was embarrassed at the notoriety given he. She blushed, then retreated to a corner where the women were sitting.

As usual, everyone clapped, but this time there was no toast to the group, as in previous years.

Julius then started the evening chat session.

"Charlie, how is the gardening business these days?"

Charlie, with his quiet demeanor, and after some consideration, gave Julius his answer.

"Good, I reckon." He stopped, and then added another statement. "Considerin' it's all under glass durin' the winter."

Julius smiled, "Well, I guess we are fortunate that some of the real gardeners, like you, are kept on, during the off season.

Charlie answered, "Yup,it shore is."

Elsie, half- listening to them, stood along with the ladies discussing "who knows what," then turned from her group and uttered a bit of humor.

"He's been there so long, they might name a plant after him."

Catherine inserted, jokingly, "They might have to plant him first."

There came the most laughter that I have heard for some time. It was wonderful, even lthough it was at poor old Charlie's expense.

He just smiled one of those quick smiles, the ones that disappear so quickly, you didn't even know it was there.

He slyly answered, "If it wasn't fer me, there just wouldn't be any spring plants ready come May, you know."

Elsie gave him that quick look, rather like a hen might look at a chick, and without blinking an eye, she gave her approval and then turned back to the lady's group and said, "Charlie has a strange sense of humor."

I think that she does sort of resemble the face of one of those chickens that I see wandering about the yard, but one wearing glasses. If I were able to laugh, I suppose I would, even though that would not be appropriate for a clock, or any person for that matter. Maybe just an inward giggle would suffice, and only inwardly since she was a very nice lady.

Julius asked his brother, "How are things at the post office Val?"

Val responded, "Going well," then he repeated himself, "yes going very well. I have just been appointed assistant to the post master."

"That's wonderful Val. I'm certain you have worked hard to attain that position."

"I have," he replied.

Mae heard their conversation, and could not resist making her own comment, so she left the lady's circle long enough to let her thoughts be known, and in her own haughty manner.

"I suppose he will soon take over as Post Master, since the one that is there is lazy and expects my poor Val to do it all!"

As though that unrequested response was not enough, she attacked her host and brother-in-law.

"Thinking about the lazy folks, how is the politician business these days?"

Not being at a loss for words, Julius looked Mae straight on, and didn't change his expression.

"The politician business is thriving nicely, thank you. I must say though, that when I think of you Mae, staying at home with your housekeeper must certainly be a hardship on you?"

Mae was shocked to be spoken to that way.

"Well I never!"

She spun around and returned to the women's group and tried to act as though she had never left them. I noticed that Val smiled, but ever so carefully.

The evening continued with the expected small talk, until the radio announced that the big ball would drop at Times Square within minutes.

Julius turned toward Molly and asked her about what she had seen, some time ago.

"You were there and saw the first one drop, didn't you Molly?"

Molly quietly replied, "Yes Julius, and it was exciting to see...especially with Don by my side."

Everyone received a refill of their glasses, and stood ready as the minutes ticked by. I was glad to gong a second or two earlier than they announced the hour. You know it does take a bit of time for the transmission of the radio waves to go from New York to Council Bluffs, where I now resided. I imagined the huge ball, that Molly described some time ago, as it was lowered down as the seconds were being counted off until midnight at Times Square. What a magnificent scene it must have been.

My gong struck midnight and each of the men kissed their wives, Anna, Claudia, and Molly gave each other a hug; the librarian watched the scenario without a partner, and then the glasses were raised as everyone said, in unison, Happy 1917! There was a slight tear in the corner of Molly's eye. No doubt, the fact that Don was not there to toast the New Year, with his New Year cry of "Here,hear" has some bearing on her sadness.

The End

Next... You will find, book three, the final chapter in my life, the "Last Move of Gilbert Clock."

Description of Factual Information given and where to find it.

(1) A Patriot's History of the United States, a book that outlines this historical event. (Also check with computer website "Wikipedia")

(2) New York in 1904 was a city on the verge of tremendous changes - and, not surprisingly, many of those changes had their genesis in the bustling energy and thronged streets of Times Square. Two innovations that would completely transform the Crossroads of the World debuted in 1904: the opening of the city's first subway line, and the first-ever celebration of New Year's Eve in Times Square. (See gonyc.about.com or google New Year
Ball Drop.)

(3) On 20 November 1913, the Paris Observatory, using the Eiffel Tower as an antenna, exchanged sustained wireless signals with the United States Naval Observatory which used an antenna in Arlington, Virginia. The object of the transmissions was to measure the difference in longitude between Paris and Washington, D.C. (Courtesy of Wikipedia – Eiffel Tower)

(4) In 1909, Chicago publisher W. D. Boyce visited London, and became lost on a foggy street
when an unknown Scout guided him to his destination. The boy explained that he was a Boy Scout and was doing his daily good turn. Upon after his return to the U.S., Boyce incorporated the Boy Scouts of America on February 8, 1910. In January 1911, the movement was turned over to James E. West who became the first Chief Scout Executive
and Scouting began to expand in the U.S. (Courtesy of Wikipedia-Boy Scouts)

(5) The 1908 New York to Paris Race was an automobile competition consisting of drivers attempting to travel from New York to Paris. This was a notable challenge given the state of automobile technology and road infrastructure at the time. Only three of six contestants completed the course. The winner was the United States team, driving a 1907 Thomas Flyer.
(Courtesy of Wikipedia. New York to Paris Race)

(6) (Morris County Library – or go to http://mclib.info/prices/1909.html)

(7)

The name "Hudson" came from Joseph L. Hudson, a Detroit department store entrepreneur and founder of Hudson's department store, who provided the necessary capital and gave permission for the company to be named after him. A total of eight Detroit businessmen formed the company on February20, 1909.
(Coutesy of Wikipedia. Hudson)

(8)

Dodge realized he had found a pass for the Union Pacific Railroad, west of the Platte River. In May 1866, he resigned from the military and, with the endorsement of Generals Grant and Sherman, became the Union Pacific's chief engineer and thus a leading figure in the construction of the Transcontinental Railroad.(Courtesy of Wikipedia – Black Jack Johnson)

(9)

Johnson became the first African American world heavyweight boxing champion (1908–1915).

(In a documentary about his life, Ken Burns notes), "for more than thirteen years, Jack Johnson was the most famous African-American on Earth."

(10)
From the book "History of Pottawattamie County, Iowa" Vol 1 by Field & Reed discusses history of grapes in Pottawattamie County and the new warehouses built by the Council Bluffs Grape Growers Association
(History of Pottawattamie County, Iowa)

(11)
African-American Willy Brown is lynched by a mob from South Omaha after being accused of raping a white woman from that neighborhood. There was a background of resentment against blacks among the ethnic and immigrant white working class in South Omaha because blacks were hired as strikebreakers. The reform mayor tried to calm the crowd; he was also lynched by the mob; only a last minute rescue saved his life.

Nebraska-born actor Henry Fonda was 14 years old when the lynching happened. His father owned a printing plant across the street from the courthouse. He watched the rfrom the second floor window of his father's shop. (Courtesy of Google.)

(12)
Thomas J. Maloney, mayor of Council Bluffs, Iowa in 1908, 1910 and 1913.
(From History of Pottawattamie County, Iowa: from the earliest historic times to 1907, Volume 2:

(13)
Sears & Roebuck Catalogue, (1908 Issue)

(14)
The new drug, formally acetylsalicylic acid, was named Aspirin by Bayer AG after the old botanical name for meadowsweet, Spiraea ulmaria. By 1899, Bayer was selling it around the world.

(15)
In 1910, the world's first commercial cargo flight occurred when one of the Wright Brothers' exhibition pilots, Phillip Parmalee, flew two packages containing 88 kilograms ofsilk from Dayton to Columbus in a Wright Model B, a distance of 70 miles (110 km).(Courtesy of Wikipedia – Columbus Ohio)

(16)
Lee De Forest (August 26, 1873 – June 30, 1961) was an American inventor with over 180 patents to his credit. De Forest invented the Audion, a vacuum tube that takes relatively weak electrical signals and amplifies them. De Forest is one of the fathers of the "electronic age," as the Audion helped to usher in the widespread use of electronics. He is also credited with one of the principal inventions which brought sound to motion pictures.
He was born in 1873 in Council Bluffs, Iowa His father was a Congregational Church minister and he accepted a position of President of Talladega College, in Talladega, Alabama. Many citizens of the white community resented his father's efforts to educate Negro students.
(Courtesy of Wikipedia – Lee DeForest)

(17)

Mother's Day was first U.S. national holiday and then later as an international holiday. It was declared officially by the state of West Virginia in 1910, and the rest of states followed quickly. On May 8, 1914, the U.S. Congress passed a law designating the second Sunday in
May as Mother's Day and requested a proclamation.
(Courtesy of Wikipedia)

(18)

By 1880, according to the New York World, Standard Oil was "the most cruel, impudent, pitiless, and grasping monopoly that ever fastened upon a country. In 1911, the Supreme Court of the United States found Standard Oil Company of New Jersey in violation of the Sherman Antitrust Act. The court ruled that the trust originated in illegal monopoly practices and ordered it to be broken up into 34 new companies.
 (Courtesy of Wikipedia –
J.D. Rockefeller Standard Oil)

(19)

Ray Harroun was born on January 12, 1879 in Spartansburg, Pennsylvania. In 1910, Harroun accepted an offer from Howard C. Marmon to design and build a racing car to be driven by him in the first big event at the new speedway at Indianapolis.

Tuesday May 30, 1911, in the car known as the Marmon Wasp.

(Courtesy of the Motorsports Hall of Fame)

(20)

On August 21, 1911, Leonardo da Vinci's Mona Lisa, one of the most famous paintings in the world ... museum director of the Louvre, approximately a year before the theft.
(Courtesy of History-1900s.about.com/od/famouscrimesscandals/a/monalisa.htm)

(21)

The Governor of New Jersey from 1911 to 1913. With Progressive ("Bull Moose") Party candidate Theodore Roosevelt and Republican nominee William Howard Taft dividing the Republican Party vote, Wilson was elected President as a Democrat in 1912. Like his archrival Republican Senator Henry Cabot Lodge,Wilson is the only president to hold a Ph.D. degree. (Courtesy of Wikipdeia – Woodrow Wilson)

(22)

With little in the way of a formal education, Louis Chevrolet learned car design while working for Buick. He built an overhead valve six-cylinder engine in his own machine shop. On November 8, 1911 Chevrolet cofounded the Chevrolet Motor Car Company with Durant (ousted from General Motors) and investment partners William Little and Dr. Edwin R. Campbell (son-in-law of Durant). The company was established in Detroit, he chose for the emblem, the stylized Swiss cross, to honor his parents' homeland. Chevrolet sold Durant his share in the company in 1915. By 1917 the Chevrolet company that Louis had cofounded was folded into General Motors. (Compliments of Wikipedia – Louis Chevrolet)

(23)

The Sixteenth Amendment (Amendment XVI) to the United States Constitution allows the Congress to levy an income tax without apportioning it among the states or basing it on Census results. This amendment exempted income taxes from the constitutional requirements regarding direct taxes, after income taxes on rents, dividends, and interest were ruled to be direct taxes in Pollock v. Farmers' Loan & Trust Co. (1895). It was ratified on February 3, 1913.

(Courtesy of Wikipedia – 16th   Amendment)

(24)
Albert Hustin (1882-1967) was a Belgian medical doctor. He was the second to   successfully practice non-direct blood transfusions with sodium citrate used as an anticoagulant. Luis Agote, from Argentina, was the first doctor to practice this kind of transfusion. (The first non-direct transfusion was performed on   March 27, 1914 by Albert Hustin with a   much diluted solution of blood. The   Argentine doctor Luis Agote used a much   less diluted solution in November of the same year.
(Courtesy of Wikipedia – Albert Hustin)

(25)
Sabath (D) of Illinois. The act (passed in July, 1913) established Federal Bureaus at   railroad junctures and stations to protect   immigrants from local nativists and to aid newly arrived immigrants to the United States who were traveling cross-country to their final destinations. The government rented buildings near the stations and equipped them with reception rooms, baths, laundry, and beds.
(Courtesy of Google – Adolph J. Sabath)

(26)
Nativism typically means opposition to immigration or efforts to lower the political or legalstatus of specific ethnic or cultural groups because the groups are considered hostile oralien to the natural culture, and it is assumed that they cannot be assimilated.
(Courtesy of Wikipedia – Nativism) – See Webster Dictionary for alternative meaning.

(27)
The Weeks-McLean Act was a law of the United States. It was sponsored by Representative John W. Weeks (R) of Massachusetts and Senator George P. McLean (R) of Connecticut. It prohibited the spring hunting and marketing of migratory birds. It also prohibited the importation of wild bird feathers for women's fashion, ending what was called "millinery murder." It gave the Secretary of Agriculture the power to set hunting seasons nationwide, making it the first U.S. law ever passed to regulate the shooting of migratory birds. It became effective on 4 March 1913 but, because of a constitutional weakness, was later replaced by the Migratory Bird Treaty Act of 1918.
(Courtesy of Wikipedia – Migratory Bird Act)

(28)
In July 1913, locals of the Western Federation of Miners called a general strike against all mines in the Michigan Copper Country. The strike was called without approval by the national WFM, after the recent strikes in the west. The union supported the strike, but faced difficulties providing pay and supplies to the strikers. Hundreds of strikers
surrounded the mine shafts to prevent others from reporting to work. Almost all mines shut down. The union demanded an 8-hour day, a minimum wage of $3 per day, an end to use of the one-man drill, and that the companies recognize it as the employees' representative (Courtesy of Wikipedia – Strikes 1913)

(29)
There were several benefits of the assembly line including:
Workers do no heavy lifting, no stooping or bending over, No special training required.
There are jobs that almost anyone can do
Provided employment to immigrants The gains in productivity allowed Ford to increase worker pay from $2.50 per day to $5.00 per day and to

reduce the hourly work week while continuously lowering the Model T price. These goals appear altruistic; however, it has been argued that they were implemented by Ford in order to reduce high employee turnover. (Courtesy of Wikipedia –Henry Ford)

(30)
A nurse by training, she was an early advocate for educating women concerning contraception. Like many contemporary feminists, she saw abortion as a tragic consequence of social conditions, and birth control as a positive alternative. (Courtesy of Wikipedia – Emma Goldman)

(31)
The toggle light switch was invented in 1916 by William J. Newton and Morris Goldberg. (Courtesy Google)

(32)
During the 1880s and 1890s, he served as president or chief engineer of dozens of railroad companies. Dodge went to New York City to manage his growing number of businesses he

had developed. Dodge returned home to Iowa and died in Council Bluffs in 1916. He is buried there in Walnut Hill Cemetery. His home, the Grenville M. Dodge House, is a National Historic
Landmark.
(Google General Grenville M. Dodge)

(33)
Marconi's Wireless Telegraph Company first developed the Mark III Short-Wave Tuner in 1915. From 1916 on, several variations of this tuner were manufactured by a number of companies, including Robert W. Paul, the W/T Factory, A.T.M. Company, and Johnson and Phillips.
(Courtesy of Wikipedia – Marconi)

(34)
WOWO started broadcasting March 31, 1925 on 500 watts, 1320 kilocycles. Call letters chosen arbitrarily. "W" for broadcast station east of the Mississippi and "O" for ease of pronunciation. A slogan erroneously traced to call letters was used for a time: "Wayne Offers Wonderful Opportunities." WOW
(Courtesy of Wikipedia – Radio Stations)

Made in the USA
Columbia, SC
09 August 2022